RED RATTLE BOOKS

MORTAL SHUFFLE

Jim Lawler lives in Liverpool. Jim Lawler learnt the hard way
about crime, criminals and the police. When young he was
convicted for criminal offences that included assault and burglary.
He is now a much more reserved and thoughtful character.

To Barbara

MORTAL SHUFFLE

JIM LAWLER

red rattle
BOOKS

Mortal Shuffle

2014

Front and back cover and
artwork by Robin Castle

Copyright © Jim Lawler

Cover image © iStock

The moral right of the
author has been asserted.

A CIP catalogue record for this book
is available from the British Library.

ISBN 978-1-909086-13-5

Printed by Ingrams Limited

www.redrattlebooks.co.uk

MORTAL SHUFFLE

1

KATE ON THE BEACH

Every night Kate ran past the metal men. They stared at the horizon and saw nothing while waves lapped at their feet.

Every night, summer or winter, sunshine or rain, she ran along Crosby beach and past the metal men. They were supposed to move the metal men after a couple of months, take them elsewhere, but the statue had proved too popular. The locals wanted the metal men to stay.

Every night Kate asked herself what was a statue, was it each of the many metal men that stood on the beach and faced the Mersey, so it was really many statues, or was it all the men together, and did that mean the statue included the space and air that separated each metal man from the other.

Every night, as Kate ran, she thought about the metal men and what the statue or statues was or were supposed to mean. At first, she had no idea. But, night after night, she sensed the space between the men and wondered about why all the metal men were identical. She thought about the same man being in a different place and each of them being seen by her in a different moment. She talked to others about the metal men and said she believed that the statue meant we are all constantly being defined and redefined by time and location. This was our freedom and our prison. What she said made sense when she ran past the metal men.

Every night Kate had moments when she worried. Her breathing would catch in her throat, and she would worry whether her physical strength was becoming less than it had been. These moments occurred every night, as did her thoughts about the women who had been raped on the beach in the past. Kate always carried a panic alarm and a small can of pepper spray. She also knew how to kick and punch. Kate was a policewoman. Nevertheless, she had these moments.

Every night Kate doubted whether she really understood what the statue meant. She was a policewoman, not an art critic. In these moments, she remembered Nathan and how he talked as if he understood everything.

Every night there would be a moment when Kate remembered Nathan.

Every night she remembered.

2

NATHAN IN THE CHURCH

I am at the funeral of a dead copper called Charlie. There are coppers everywhere. It is ridiculous. The funeral is so busy, the coppers have been asked to use the annexe, which has been wired with a loudspeaker. I stand apart from the others but say hello to people. We each manage a sentence before they move on. They usually ask me if I have seen Carl. It is an excuse for them to not stay. I point him out. He is standing in front of the church entrance and he is grinning at people. The policemen in uniform all stand close to Carl. He holds a peaked cap and gloves in his left hand. Some detectives are talking to visitors. In the fresh air the voices are faint, sound more polite than normal. I pretend to be occupied.

I take my obituary out of my wallet. I read my obituary.

'Today, Cheshire Constabulary accepted that its esteemed colleague, Nathan Wrench, has probably been murdered. 'We are now treating his disappearance as a definite killing,' said an obviously emotional Detective Inspector Douglas Franklin. 'Witnesses saw Nathan shot in the chest and have testified that members of the gang carried a badly injured Nathan away from the scene of their crime. A week ago, Adbury police station received a message that stated Nathan was already dead. Unfortunately, I can't share the details of that message with the press because of its obscene nature. In the two weeks since his disappearance we have received no evidence of Nathan being given medical treatment for the injuries he sustained.' Detective Sergeant Nathan Wrench turned just thirty years old last September.'

There is more. No one needs to know, I say to myself.

Above the obituary, there is a photo of me, fresh faced and in uniform. I am dark and handsome. I have a daft smile on my face. I put the obituary back into my wallet.

A dark-blue car turns through the tall gates at the front of the cemetery. The January day is dry and bright and not even cold. Mourners stand around on the edge of the tarmac drive that leads to the church. Most wait by their parked cars. The dark-blue car stops and parks by the edge of the drive. The church at the end of the tarmac is modern and average. The graveyard, which is older, is enormous.

Carl stops smiling at someone and walks towards me.

'There won't be enough seats, Nathan,' he says. 'This is strange. I didn't know Charlie was so popular.'

'He did no harm,' I say. 'You look the part, Carl, in the extra braid.'

'I think I look all right,' he says. 'I've lost weight, Nathan. The personal trainer is working.'

Carl is popular with the women. He smiles a lot.

'Christ, you must hate funerals,' says Carl.

I say nothing.

Carl knows when he is just talking. Two uniformed policemen, standing in front of the church entrance, nod hello at Carl. He raises his thumb.

Another car crawls into the cemetery. Carl catches their attention and waves a hand. The hand that holds his peaked cap and gloves stays at his side.

'How on earth did you ever make Superintendent?' I say.

'It must have been fate,' he says. 'Are you all right today, Nathan?'

'Of course,' I say.

'There's no of course about it, Nathan. What does Doctor Long think?'

'She says I'm alright.'

'What about Esther?'

'She is in Spain,' I say.

'I know that,' he says. 'Are you and Esther all right?'

'Of course,' I say.

'Alex doesn't like it at all.'

'I know that. Why should I care what Alex likes?'

'Because we have to,' says Carl.

'I do not care,' I say.

I stare at the gravestones behind the wall. The graveyard must stretch at least a mile.

'`All in chains waiting to be butchered`,' I say, 'Pascal.'

Carl says nothing. He does not speak whenever I quote a book or someone.

'Why is nobody going inside the church?' I say.

'They're waiting for the family. This isn't genuine grief, Nathan. These are just distant relatives and friends.'

'I thought you looked quite concerned.'

'I'm doing my best.'

Carl smiles.

More cars come into the cemetery, and more mourners stand by. The long tarmac drive is crowded. Three black limousines stop in a line in front of the entrance to the church. Tyres rest, engines become quiet and waiting mourners take a breath. Carl and me watch without saying anything. Some of the other mourners go inside the church.

Carl sighs. He looks at me.

'You should have had the career, Nathan,' he says.

'After the kidnap, I lost interest,' I say.

'Nathan, you don't have to be interested. Look at me.'

'I'm cleverer and prettier but it's been a long time since it's been about that. You are liked, Carl. You know how to influence.'

'You used to work hard,' he says.

'I thought I could be a hero,' I say. 'I haven't thought that for a while.'

Relatives of the deceased leave the limousines. The wife and two brothers cry together. A teenage son that looks like Dracula puts his arm around the wife but the vampire cries as well. A white Toyota is parked close by. Dracula has skin the same colour as the nearby Toyota. He wears dark glasses, and his tears seep below the frames. He would be popular with vampire fans, I think. Two men in authentic funeral suits lower the coffin on to the low trolley next to a limousine. They hold the coffin to stop it sliding.

"Ere you be old, learn to live and pray',' I say.

Carl says nothing.

'It's Thackeray,' I say, '*Vanity Fair*.'

Carl says nothing.

'I walked out on my kids,' I say. 'I had to pay a price, I guess.'

'It's all that sodding reading. I hope it's a comfort, Nathan.'

'Why should I have comfort?'

We watch the coffin be wheeled into the church. The family follows the coffin inside. Frail sad figures with faces all pale anguish. Their sobs can be still heard after they disappear. Others follow the relatives and friends into the church. The policemen are directed into the annexe next door. Carl stands up straight. He has a strange complexion that resembles red wine bleached with milk, and his curly hair is a peculiar mix of yellow and white, as if the milk on his face has turned sour on top of his head. Despite it all, he looks very clean. Everyone knows that his mother taught him good habits. I suspect Carl uses very hot showers. He wears two rings on his fingers, and it looks odd on a Superintendent in full uniform.

Carl and me walk and talk.

'These things are never pleasant,' he says. 'I had a high opinion of Charlie. Poor bugger dropped down dead by the swimming pool, a couple of months off his pension and fit as a fiddle. No good life for Charlie. All I hope is I don't get emotional, and you don't either, Nathan.'

'Why should I be emotional about Charlie?' I say.

'I don't mean Charlie,' says Carl. 'Come on, bright boy.'

We hesitate in front of the annexe.

'Do they have a video in this?' I say

'Just loudspeakers, I think,' says Carl.

'They could do it on video,' I say.

We listen to familiar organ notes.

'I feel sorry for his family,' says Carl.

I am not sure that I believe this.

'First time I've ever mourned in an annexe,' says Carl.

I can believe that.

We step through the doorway of the annexe to the church.

Inside the annexe, everybody stands close together. There are no seats. We hear the vicar through the loudspeaker. He mentions the Kingdom and the heart of God.

I whisper into the ear of Carl. 'The physical trainer is having an effect. That uniform used to be tight.'

'I do a lot of running,' says Carl.

'I can't run. I've a bad back.'

'Since the kidnap?'

'Since the kidnap,' I say.

The voice on the loudspeaker talks about Charlie as if he was something special and not really dead. The people in the annexe listen to the loudspeaker as if they have hope and believe in the voice. I imagine the other mourners, out of sight in the real church with the real vicar.

"This wonderful thing we all do',' I say.

Carl says nothing. He already looks emotional.

'Dying, Henry James said it in a book somewhere,' I explain.

Carl says nothing, wipes something moist from his eye.

3

NATHAN VISITING ESTHER

I am standing outside the home of Esther. The man across the road is being insensitive. This is not the day to paint his house. He is painting the upstairs window. My white Ford Fiesta is parked where I normally leave it, on the pavement in front of her garden. The Fiesta is unlocked. I trust the neighbours because they are rich. I do not really trust them. I just do not expect them to steal cars. The Cheshire winter weather is still warm and dry.

I am dressed smartly. I wear a jacket and trousers for my work. Sometimes I even wear a tie. This is unusual for a detective. Esther opens the door. She is suntanned and looks even more beautiful than when she left two weeks ago for Spain.

The neighbour waves his paintbrush and shouts hello to Esther.

'He's a dickhead,' says Esther.

'He shouldn't be painting,' I say.

'I hope he falls off his fucking ladder,' says Esther.

She is tired and emotional, and I know why. Somebody has painted her house yellow, all of it, the windows, the window frames, the door and the bricks. Unusual it is, stylish it is not.

'I hope he falls off that ladder,' says Esther. 'Can't you arrest him?'

I say nothing and let Esther be angry.

A brown and white cat snuggles up against her legs. This is understandable. Most would like to snuggle against those legs.

'I've missed you,' I say. 'I was looking forward to seeing you.'

She is slow to let me into the house. She wants me to stand

and stare at her house painted yellow. She lifts the cat and holds it against her chest.

'Great, isn't it?' she says. 'What a mess.'

I watch the cat snuggle in close against her breasts. I think of soft yielding footballs.

'I thought you would have rung me before the police,' I say.

'I knew what you'd want if I'd called you.'

She is right, of course. I would have taken her to bed and called the council afterwards about removing the paint.

Esther scratches her neck, and the cat fidgets and yawns. Esther strokes the cat. To act sympathetically, I look at the yellow paint again. Even though there are streaks and the house has been painted quickly, there is a lot of yellow paint.

At the head of the cul-de-sac a group of small children play together. I listen to them. The voices are indistinct but happy. Together they make a noise that sounds like waves lapping against rocks. I have been hearing peculiar noises all morning but this is not unusual. I have been strange for some time. I watch the children play. They all stand very erect, as if they are pretending to be famous.

Esther taps me on the shoulder.

'Fed up already?' she says.

'I was waiting for you to say something.'

'No you weren't. You were watching the kids.'

I look at the house again.

'What is the point of the yellow paint?' I say.

'Why yellow?' says Esther.

'Yes,' I say.

Esther strokes the cat again. She still will not let me into the house. I could force my way in but I would like to be welcomed. I turn my back on her and watch the children swap places and exchange orders. Two of the children act as the leaders. The rest sit on the edge of the pavement, all next to one another. They have small chins and big grins. I look at the yellow paint again.

'It could have been worse,' I say. 'We'll get the paint off.'

I am trying to be supportive but Esther scowls. I want to go inside. Esther is beautiful, and I have missed her, well, I have missed something. Esther is younger than me but not by much. I do not like women too young. I have had young girlfriends but, when that happens, I look in the mirror every day for signs of ageing. Esther is late thirties. She has strong eyes and cheekbones. Her smiles always make me feel flattered. Her figure impresses everyone, classic curves and soft and subtle padding that entices. The cat lines its spine along the gap between the soft yielding footballs. I envy the cat. Alex McGrath is rarely complimentary about Esther but he did once admit under pressure from Carl that she was glamorous.

I stare at Esther. She has more than glamour. Her body is perfect and complete. If only we thought alike, I tell myself, still, that beauty. I feel that I should honour her by missing the occasional breath.

'Any idea where they may have found the paint?' I say.

'Ah,' she says, 'you're going to be a policeman. They should have sent a proper policeman, not you, Nathan.'

'It looks like yellow undercoat,' I say.

'It looks worse from the inside. It looks like global warming in there.'

Esther points to inside her house.

'You can tell it's undercoat,' I say. 'That's why it's so streaky. They would not have had time for two coats. It is terrible what people do. I can understand why you are upset.'

Esther points to the neighbour on the ladder.

'He saw my new paint and couldn't resist,' she says.

'I have never seen anything like this to be honest. Let me inside the house, and I'll phone the council to get it cleaned.'

'You can phone them from your mobile.'

Esther is being unfriendly. I had been expecting a present from Spain. She bends her head down and uses her chin to stroke the head of the cat.

'Alex thinks he's clever,' she says.

She throws the cat back inside the house. The children on the pavement carry on playing. I listen to them laugh. I imagine I hear giggles and happiness. I look at the yellow paint again. The winter sun has disappeared behind a cloud, and the house looks worse than ever.

Still trying to be helpful, I speak. 'You'll be able to claim it on the insurance, I think. You can quote my name on the claim form.'

'They should have sent me a proper policeman. Somebody independent. I haven't unpacked or anything. I was hoping to make some phone calls this afternoon.'

'The business will look after itself.'

'What do you know,' says Esther.

To look as if I have expertise, I walk over to the garage doors. I have a decent look. I am not sure what I am doing or even what I look like I am doing.

'This is definitely undercoat,' I say.

'I don't deserve this,' says Esther. 'It's just as well that the car was parked at the airport for a fortnight.'

Esther can only talk about cars for so long. She walks inside her house and, presuming I have been humiliated enough, I follow her all the way to the living room. Despite the yellow paint outside, the living room is admirable but then it does reflect my traditional taste; pink walls, a fine wooden fireplace, the two comfortable sofas on top of expensive Afghanistan rugs and quality curtains brushing against the thick pile carpet that borders the rugs. I am an influence.

The patio window at the back of the house has also been painted yellow. I walk up to the yellow windows. I press my fingers against the glass. Esther switches on a light. I tell myself that she is trying to be helpful.

'It's the whole house,' I say.

'I know it's the whole house.'

'Jesus,' I say.

Esther sits down on one of her sofas. I walk over to the fine wooden fireplace and watch Esther cross her legs. The lines of her legs look as fine as lines drawn by a pencil. I imagine a pencil sliding smoothly over the paper.

'What was it like?' I say.

'Seeing the house yellow?' she says.

'No, your holiday in Gran Canaria.'

'It was a break. I needed a break. I didn't do anything.'

'I missed you. When you are not there, I think about you. I know I'm always reading but I like you to be there with me.'

'It wasn't your kind of holiday.'

'No,' I say.

'This from Alex has gone on long enough, Nathan. You probably think it's funny.'

I pause.

'You have clearly upset somebody,' I say.

'Not somebody, Nathan, it's Alex, Alex McGrath, I'm being pressurised. I was getting phone calls while I was on holiday.'

'This is the first time I have heard about unpleasant telephone calls. I was unaware.'

'Why should I tell you? You never rang anyway.'

'You never rang me, either'

'No,' she says.

'You have a nice tan.'

'I tan easily.'

'I know you do. The sun worships you.'

'I wouldn't sunbathe if I got freckles. I've half a dozen sun beds in my gym.'

'Alex hates New Beginnings.'

'New Beginnings For Hurting Bodies,' Esther corrects me.

'The name is unusual.'

'I wanted something that sounded spiritual. Well-being, you know. I've only just cleaned the paint off those walls. My customers seeing that wasn't right.'

'Alex has been saying things about the girls who work there.'

'They're honest girls.'

'People say they're fit and look the part. I suppose you have to.'

'I supply personal trainers. I give a free New Beginnings T shirt. What's Alex going to paint next? Me, I expect. No doubt you think you deserve a cup of tea?'

A cup of tea could lead to something. I sit down.

'Shouldn't you take some notes?' says Esther.

I pull a notebook and pen out of my shirt pocket. I write down the date and the address and read it. For some reason, this makes Esther smile.

'You always look less mad when you're reading,' she says. 'But I also like your slightly mad eyes. Those and your dark thick hair.'

I smile.

'I like it when you smile,' she says. 'It's like an apology for something.'

Esther has said this before. I have smiled at myself in the mirror to see what she means. I think she may have a point.

'I'll make some tea,' says Esther.

I follow Esther into the kitchen. I study her body from behind, admire again curves toned with athleticism and grace. I imagine myself all alone in the middle of her warmth.

In the kitchen, I put down my notebook and pen on one of the work surfaces. Like all the others, the kitchen windows are painted yellow.

Esther boils a kettle and finds cups.

'I should have been in work by now,' she says.

Esther pours boiling water. We stand either side of the boiling kettle.

'You still need to empty your suitcases,' I say.

'Later,' she says. 'I'm not thinking properly.'

I pull the cup of tea towards me.

'I only bought the house because I thought it was quiet,' she says. 'Next door is a doctor.'

Esther drinks her tea.

I stare at the yellow windows and say, 'It might be a neighbour after all.'

'Nathan, I know who it is. It's Alex McGrath. Remember him? You feed him information. I'm entitled to an honest enquiry.'

'Barrel Park Centre now has a full size swimming pool. Alex is proud of his hotel.'

'New Beginnings hasn't any space for a swimming pool.'

Esther sips her tea.

'I'm sorry,' she says. 'I haven't any biscuits. I've been on holiday. McGrath has wanted me out of town from the beginning'

'A bit like Franco after they elected the Republican Government,' I say.

'Nathan, shut up and drink your tea. McGrath wants it so I can't show my face. You've phoned the police in Leeds, Nathan, haven't you? How much does Alex pay you to collect dirt?'

'I have no appetite anyway,' I say.

I am thinking briefly about the biscuits. I stop thinking about biscuits.

'Are you making an allegation?' I say.

'Of course I am,' says Esther. 'Oh, Nathan, be a man.'

I drink my tea and feel anything but manly. I imagine complications between me, Carl and Alex.

'I would hate you to make unfounded allegations,' I say.

Esther puts her mug down next to the one I am using. I notice that the two mugs touch. I wait for Esther to speak.

'Tell McGrath I'm not moving,' she says. 'Tell him he needs the competition.'

'You want me to get involved or do you want me to investigate your complaint?'

'I want you to do both. I want you to be a decent copper for your sake and a decent boyfriend for my sake.'

Esther rarely calls me her boyfriend, and I do not call her my girlfriend. I suppose it is age, really.

I move my cup away so it stands by itself.

I can hear me sigh as I speak.

'Alex McGrath has put money into Adbury. He is popular and he is a reformed character.'

'He still controls the drugs, Nathan.'

'True,' I say, 'but he satisfies demand. He does not stimulate demand like some drug dealers. Thanks to McGrath, we don't have dealers waiting outside the school gates or marauding the estates.'

This, I can also vouch.

'You'll be nominating him for a knighthood next,' says Esther.

'When you see the size of his swimming pool,' I say. 'He hasn't had much luck with his dance floor, though.'

Alex McGrath owns the Barrel Park Hotel and Leisure Centre. Maybe, eventually, people will want to live there forever.

I read the side of the cup Esther uses. The comments regarding men are unflattering.

'I sometimes wish I'd never left Leeds,' says Esther. 'Sometimes I wouldn't mind being like you, born and bred. And then sometimes I hate you for it.'

Esther looks around her kitchen. The yellow windows make things between us different, undoubtedly. Eventually, she points at a photograph of Sharon Stone pinned against a cupboard. I hate this photograph because it makes me think of the moments when Esther, for all her competence, can talk like an idiot.

'Sharon Stone,' says Esther, 'I think she's beautiful. I like the way she set out to get rich and now she's all classy.'

I remember watching *Basic Instinct* with Carl one night when his mother had been staying over with his sister. The woman is definitely not ugly.

'I'd love to be blonde,' says Esther.

Here we go, I think.

'I used to hate my hair,' she says. 'I'm really ginger.'

'I know that,' I say.

Of course, I do.

'Soon as I was fifteen, I dyed it blonde,' says Esther. 'Not quite like Sharon, I bet you'd like a biscuit.'

I think of Sharon Stone opening her legs inside the police station.

'I do like something to nibble on,' I say.

I look again at the photograph of Sharon Stone.

'Carl has a personal trainer who shouts at him when he puts on weight,' I say.

'He'd take it the wrong way,' says Esther. 'My girls wouldn't shout at anyone. In small towns, people surrender to bad habits. All the men have paunches.'

Esther sips some tea.

'Which is why I'm here in Adbury,' she says. 'To make them all fit again. The fitter they get the cheaper it is for them.'

'It still costs time.'

'They have to spend it somewhere. Why do I have to leave Adbury? Will you be proud of yourself then, Nathan? When I'm downtrodden.'

'I will talk to Alex.'

The idea makes me uneasy.

'I shall have to speak to all the neighbours,' I say.

This I imagine with less dread.

'For clues?' says Esther.

'Clues?' I say.

I do not normally think about clues.

'Something Alex said that might be incriminating,' says Esther.

Clues? The idea is hilarious. Esther will have me making real notes next.

'Just go and see Alex McGrath,' she says.

'I intend to talk to the neighbours first,' I say. 'Nothing equals finding a witness.'

'You haven't written much in your notebook.'

I stare at the notebook. Esther is right, and I am embarrassed. The two mugs of tea are both empty.

'Yellow paint,' I say, probably because I am surrounded by the stuff. 'What does it mean?'

'Alex McGrath has mates,' says Esther.

'He is popular.'

'He is with you lot. Sucking up to him. Doing his dirty business.'

'I'll talk to Alex.'

'Aye.'

Esther picks up the two cups, holds them aloft with one finger.

'Don't creep, Nathan,' she says. 'Tell him we know it's him.'

'We won't trace this back to Alex McGrath,' I say.

Esther raises the hand with the two cups.

I step back and say, 'I will talk to Alex McGrath. I will do what you say. I will also look for clues.'

'Clues?' says Esther.

'I will have a good look around.'

'It's not the neighbours. I'm going to have to complain about all this. You're taking the piss, Nathan.'

'If you have concerns you would like me to pass on to my superior officer.'

'He'll be as daft as you. You need somebody to say something. A complaint might do you a favour.'

Esther is daft enough to complain. She is always being critical of me, insisting that I need to become disciplined. We are agreed that this is desirable. What we do not agree on is the date when such plans can be implemented.

The kitchen door slides open, and the brown and white cat enters the kitchen on tiptoe. The cat climbs up a cupboard and on to one of the work surfaces. Before it settles the cat rubs its back against the toaster. Esther shoos the cat off the work surface. It runs along the edge of the stainless steel sink. The cat jumps off a cupboard and lands in the middle of the floor. The cat stays there and licks itself.

'I've missed you,' I say.

'I've bought you a present,' says Esther.

I phone the council and fix a date for Environmental Health to remove the paint. I phone Alex and tell him that I need to see him. Esther stands next to me and listens. We then go to bed and, well, you can imagine.

4

NATHAN IN THE STEAM ROOM

I am sitting in a sauna in the Barrel Park Hotel and Leisure Centre. There is steam everywhere.

'You came here on the bounce,' says Alex McGrath.

He is hiding behind the steam somewhere except he is not really hiding. I am the one who prefers not to be seen.

'I came here in response to a complaint to the police,' I say.

Alex McGrath is sitting opposite me on a blue fibreglass bench. I can see his feet and his ankles. The walls and floors of the steam room are painted the same ice blue as the fibreglass bench.

'Some people would have taken offence,' says Alex McGrath. 'Tell me what I do. I take you for a sauna.'

My whole body is damp. I am not sure what is sweat and what is moisturized air. We had walked into the sauna wearing identical white towels. I assume Alex McGrath is still wearing his towel, as I am. I hope so.

'Drink some more water,' says McGrath.

I stare into the steam, not because I want to see the form of Alex McGrath. In a steam room all you can do is look at the steam, and your own sweat, of course.

'This is doing you good,' says Alex McGrath.

I had forgotten that in a steam room you could also be bullied by people like Alex McGrath. The wet hair on my legs is as black as liquorice.

'It will go on the rates,' I say.

'What are you taking about, Nathan,' says Alex McGrath.

'The council are sending someone to scrub off the yellow paint.'

'I don't paint houses yellow,' says McGrath.

'Esther thinks you did.'

'You and Esther,' says Alex McGrath. 'I know you and her talk some right shite. You like talking to my enemies about me.'

I ignore the insult. The visit has been pointless. Anyone who can persuade me to take a sauna is not going to listen to me.

'Drink some more water,' says McGrath.

'I once saw this horror film, and the more the hero sweated the more he bled.'

'I saw that.'

'I remember it being very touching.'

'I don't remember that,' says McGrath. 'Drink more water.'

'Can't you just leave her be?' I say.

'She's a disfigurement on the town.'

'So is her house after what you did.'

'You're going on, Nathan.'

My eyes are adjusting to the steam. I can see some of the body of Alex McGrath. The white towel, which he is still wearing, is visible.

'How was the funeral?' he says.

'Good turn out, Alex,' I say. 'Too many for the church.'

'They need a bigger church then.'

'It is embarrassing when that happens. I assume it was not just me that was embarrassed.'

I stare at the damp hair on my legs. I am not trying to drag out the conversation but the visit. I want us to say as little as possible while I am there. I touch a couple of the scars left by my kidnappers seven years earlier. Since then the scars have turned into thin strips of soft skin. Esther likes to prod them with her fingers.

'Right now the sweat is running down the back of my leg,' I say.

'Drink more water,' says Alex McGrath.

I can see enough through the steam to realise Alex McGrath is attempting to read his watch. I have hopes that this will be soon over. He scratches his arm.

'This watch is making me itch,' he says. 'I don't feel right without my waterproof watch. The time goes so slow in here.'

'Don't ever think about meditating on a mountain,' I say.

Alex McGrath bends forward and stares at my body. He appears to be looking at my legs.

'We make more money on the hair removal service than anything,' he says. 'Best thing I ever introduced.'

This makes me itch. I scratch but it is ineffectual because of the sweat and damp.

'No point in having muscles if you can't see them,' says Alex McGrath.

I lean back into the corner, hoping that my face will disappear into the steam.

'All bodily hair?' I say.

'Arseholes are extra,' says Alex McGrath.

'Surely that would lead to infection?'

'Esther only does the cream. We have a machine. We don't do arseholes, though.' Alex pauses to reconsider. 'We could do arseholes if they wanted.'

'Esther might be doing them already.'

'She only sells cream, Nathan. She doesn't provide a real hair removal service. She doesn't provide a swimming pool or even a steam room. Believe me. Steam rooms don't come much hotter than this.'

I keep my head out of sight in the steam filled corner.

Although timid, I can be controversial which is why I probably say, 'Before I was a copper, I once worked in a brewery. They had a huge oven to roast the barley or something. Every so often we had to go and turn this barley over in the oven. We were only allowed in for three minutes. That was hot.'

'It wasn't hotter than this.'

'Alex, it was an oven. On what basis can you compare?'

I hear him grunt. I am too tired to argue, especially after the conversation about the yellow paint and Esther. I try a compliment.

'Alex, Barrel Park is fabulous. There has never been anything like Barrel Park in Adbury.'

It's merit we can debate another day, I think. Alex McGrath has a troubled expression. The steam is still there, everywhere in fact, but he looks at me as if it does not exist.

'You will make a fortune, Alex,' I say.

'It's been a long time coming, Nathan,' he says. 'No wonder I get depressed.'

'I doubt if you are the type.'

'Let me tell you. I've had to go for counselling.'

McGrath forgets about me and watches the steam move around instead.

'Avril insisted,' he says.

Ah, he was remembering.

'When was this?' I say.

'Just before I dumped her.'

'Carl believes that you are better off without Avril.'

'I miss her, Nathan. You don't go to counselling if you don't care. Avril was sincere but she realised the violence in our relationship was causing me pain.'

'I never suspected she hit you, Alex.'

'She didn't, Nathan. I hit her.'

McGrath looks at his two bare wet feet. I suppose he had to eventually. I think about his feet as well. I find it difficult to imagine these feet inside shoes and Alex using them to kick people.

'You don't have to tell me,' he says. 'I'm better off without her, Nathan. Avril was a very appreciative woman but, believe me, she had a strong sense of what was right and wrong. She couldn't be told.'

Knowing Alex McGrath, that would have been difficult, I think.

'Listen to this, Nathan. Of every four days everyone works, the money from one day goes back to the banks to pay off debt. I read that.'

'I have no real talent for money, Alex.'

'Drink more water, Nathan; imagine me, someone trying to transform Adbury. You don't realise. The sensible don't have loans and mortgages.'

I think about the word sensible but I am too preoccupied with what he might say and do next to worry about his intention with the word sensible.

'I hate that High Street,' he says. 'I hate New Beginnings. I hate Esther. And I hate that Little Picture House. I'd flatten that, at least. Nobody has ever heard of the films.'

'New Beginnings is a pokey gym'. You take it too seriously.'

'I was told it was just going to be sun beds. It was supposed to be called Island Paradise. Just sunbathing. She's providing personal trainers now.'

I am only half-listening. I think about our conversation and how little of it had been about what has happened to Esther. I wish I had said more. I touch my arm. My skin is damp but warmer than I expect.

'You'll never make money without faith,' says Alex McGrath. He bites a fingernail and shouts. 'You never achieve anything without faith.'

'Why would you hit Avril?' I say.

I am curious. It might be a clue to something.

'Felt like it,' he says. 'The counsellor said we're all alone really.'

'But you are there, Alex. I know because I can almost see you. And I'm here, Alex. I have to be because you insist.'

'You've done all right out of Barrel Park, free treatment, free booze and free swims in the pool. Drink your water.'

'It is a fabulous pool, Alex.'

It's definitely big, I think.

'You should behave yourself, Nathan. You don't do anybody any favours. You're not a plain man. You don't have to settle for Esther. You should be loyal.'

We have been in the sauna for at least twenty minutes. I watch Alex scratch his arm and pull out the silver strap on his waterproof watch. I rub the sweat and moisture on my arms, wipe my hands on the towel wrapped around my stomach.

'It would be funny if we died of dehydration wondering what time it was,' I say. 'After a while, you stop feeling any wetter.'

'Nathan, I'm talking about loyalty,' he says.

'Twenty minutes could be defined as loyal, Alex.'

'I'm talking about more than twenty minutes.'

'Half an hour?'

'Sticking together, Nathan, is what I'm talking about.' McGrath prises his back from the wall. 'You won't know. I thumped my father when I was fourteen, proud of myself because I had a decent right cross. Made an awful mess of his face. We were both different after that. You may be fit, Nathan, but you're not healthy. There's only so much good you can do yourself in a swimming pool. You should have regular check ups, Nathan.'

I wonder if you can die from listening to dull people with too much money and power.

'You can't do whatever you want,' says Alex McGrath.

He walks across and sits down next to me, close enough for us both to see one another properly. There are worse things than dullness, I think.

'Nathan, listen to me,' says Alex McGrath.

'Is it essential you sit that close, Alex?' I say.

'I want to make a point.'

McGrath puts his hand on my knee. The towel is drier than he expects. Something makes him look at it oddly.

'I want to throw my weight about,' says Alex McGrath.

He has had the practice, I think.

'I've just about had my fill of unreasonable people,' he says. 'It tires me.'

He does not look tired, anything but.

'I guess I feel like that most days,' I say.

I think I understand tiredness as well as anyone. I really want to put my head back in the corner.

'You're too young to understand, Nathan,' says Alex McGrath. 'You think excitement is the answer. I know it isn't.'

I sigh and say, 'The consolation of the orgasm. I always suspected it would be insufficient.'

'Shut up, Nathan. You've got years ahead of you. You have to have options, Nathan. Am I clear? Of course I am.'

Alex McGrath stares at me without blinking.

'There appears to be a problem, Alex?' I say.

'The problem is Esther,' he says.

'Esther?'

'Esther, Nathan.'

'Esther?'

'Yes, Esther.'

I sit still because I realise that moving my body may be just as bad an idea as opening my mouth.

'You know Esther, Nathan,' says Alex McGrath. 'She has that twat you've been poking.'

'That Esther,' I say. 'Twat Esther.'

'Nathan, everybody knows you're clever. So don't treat me like a fucking idiot.'

'She is entitled to socialise.'

'Of course she is, Nathan.'

I stay quiet. Right now I would prefer more steam in the room.

'Esther is entitled to see men,' he says. 'Men, Nathan, not you.'

Alex McGrath puts his hand on my thigh.

I stare at the hand but say nothing. I realise McGrath is not being friendly. Whatever the problems, Alex McGrath and me do not misunderstand one another.

'Esther is my enemy, and you have obligations,' he says. 'You will understand, Nathan. I am going to insist.'

McGrath digs his fingers into the towel on my thigh.

'And you don't come here asking questions about who painted her house yellow,' he says.

I feel his fingers press into my muscle.

'That gang who grabbed you pumped you full of shite,' says Alex McGrath.

'That was a long time ago,' I say.

'You must have had withdrawal symptoms, Nathan.'

'Enough not to go through it again.'

'I don't care how fucking far you can swim in the pool. You've got problems.'

'It is a fabulous pool, Alex.'

'I'm proud of it. Esther would be happier if she didn't see you.'

'I'll ask Esther. I'm not convinced.'

'I say this.'

I am not sure what that means but he said it. It sounded like someone talking in an epic film.

'Can I have a shower now?' I say.

Perhaps afterwards we can return to normal conversation or something like normal.

'Shut up, Nathan?' says Alex McGrath. 'Has Carl asked you to have this word?'

'I'm here on behalf of Esther,' I say.

'You piece of dirt,' says Alex McGrath.

He takes his hand off my thigh.

'I could fucking destroy you if I wanted,' he says,

'You're swearing a lot, Alex,' I say.

'I wouldn't even have to break sweat.'

This I do not doubt. I say nothing.

'I don't mind your humour, Nathan,' says Alex McGrath.

Have I just cracked a joke without actually saying anything? This could be a first.

'It's your argumentative nature I dislike,' says Alex McGrath. 'You owe me, Nathan. You spend more than you earn. I'm disappointed you've nothing to show for it. I've helped you. I don't blame myself.'

'I have a decent house.'

'Nothing but books and DVDs.'

'I am cutting down on the books. I can't remember what I read anymore, anyway. Can I have a shower?'

McGrath presses his thighs against me. He forces me along the edge of the ice-blue fibreglass bench. Steam moves politely out of the way. McGrath closes his hands into fists.

'You've kept in shape, Nathan,' he says. 'My pool is doing you good.'

Alex McGrath touches one of my muscles.

'I know Esther encourages you,' he says.

I grip the edge of the fibreglass bench. The damp air helps my hands stick to the seat. McGrath covers one of my fists with one of his hands.

'Have you done much rough stuff, Nathan?' says Alex McGrath.

'It's not quite how we see modern policing,' I say.

I regret the remark almost immediately.

With the hand not touching me, he hits the side of my head and grabs me by the back of the neck. I am pulled all the way down to the concrete floor. My face is pressed hard against the warm damp concrete. I think of the final moments of Janet Leigh in the movie, *Psycho*. I am not in the best of spirits. Alex McGrath has dropped down beside me. He wedges his knee against the side of my head. The concrete is sharp against my face. My sweat and the steam are no help at all. I tell myself that I will probably live through this but at the moment I am being pinned to the floor by someone who thought it a good idea to paint a house in yellow undercoat. I have doubts.

'Don't move, Nathan,' says the someone that paints houses in yellow undercoat. 'I wouldn't want to rub your face off. You listen to me.'

'I think I get the point, Alex.' I mumble rather than speak clearly.

'I'll make sure you do. You're not going to be difficult anymore. Nathan, I'm in no mood for a violent saga.'

This sounds promising. I hope so. McGrath bends all the way

over until his head is level with mine. He looks into the eye that I have pressed down on the concrete floor.

'You all right down there?' he says.

'Not really, Alex,' I am still mumbling.

'I won't have any misunderstandings.' McGrath presses his knee down on my back. 'Do we want misunderstandings?'

'Certainly not.'

'Just so you believe me.'

McGrath butts the back of my head. I know this because I hear an awfully close bang and I feel a lot of pain. The concrete floor becomes different. The flat surface turns into sharp ridges that dig into my face. Two ridges in particular are pressing against my eye.

'You believe me now, Nathan?' says Alex McGrath.

'I have a headache, Alex,' I say. The floor muffles my words. I am not really mumbling. 'I had a headache already. I think I'm going to be sick.'

'Nathan, note I'm all right. You don't worry about me. You don't talk about me. You don't think Esther is your way out. You will be loyal. I once used to practise butting telegraph poles.'

Even imprisoned as I am by his superior strength, this is such an absurd hobby I am incapable of admiration.

'I'm good, aren't I?' says Alex McGrath.

Good? Surely not, he butts telegraph poles. I do not have contempt, though. Please let me go, Alex, I pray.

'I walked into rooms and terrified people,' says Alex McGrath. 'You were probably reading books about then.'

Well, I wasn't butting telegraph poles. All that passed me by.

'This is me being friendly, Nathan,' he says. 'You will be loyal. We are all on the same side now. You understand that I'm a serious person. I don't want to talk about yellow paint. Get up, Nathan. I hate to see you like that.'

McGrath takes his knee away from my head. I haul myself up into a sitting position. McGrath returns to the bench opposite me. The side of my head is sore. I suspect that I have a bruise.

'Do you believe I'm serious?' says Alex McGrath.

'Serious intent as opposed to intellectually curious?' I say.

Sometimes, I cannot help myself. It is like there is an emergency exit at the side of my mouth and the words just slide out while my brain is at the main entrance.

'You just take it easy,' says Alex McGrath. He is relaxed and friendly. 'You just do as you're told.'

How many bastards are out there, I do not know. All I know is that there is nothing worse than having one in your own world. I do not give advice quite like Alex McGrath but I urge all to avoid them.

5

NATHAN IS IN A GYMNASIUM TALKING TO OTHERS

I am standing with my back to a long window that overlooks the High Street. I do not want to look at the High Street because not only is there not that much to look at but Alex McGrath has left a substantial bruise on my head. For the moment, I want to avoid looking at reflections of my face.

I am here because Alex McGrath has summoned me. He is sitting opposite me on an exercise bench. Esther is standing next to him. Esther leans back against an unused exercise bike. She rests a foot on one of the still pedals. She rocks a baby buggy with her right hand. The baby inside the buggy has a face puffed up like candyfloss. Alex McGrath looks down at the fat baby and pulls his favourite face, pushes out his bottom lip with his tongue. The mouth of the baby trembles, and the small eyes fill with horror.

Esther tickles the baby under the chin, long enough for the baby to recover.

'He doesn't like monsters poking their noses in his face,' she says. 'Babies don't.'

Nearby, the mother of the baby pedals away on another exercise bike. She chews gum and speaks to her friend at the same time. The baby in the buggy raises invisible eyebrows. The face is fat enough for a wrinkle to look uncomfortable. Without using his hands, the baby twirls the dummy around his mouth.

'Very good,' says Esther.

'It's not that clever,' says Alex McGrath.

Esther is wearing a black sweatshirt over grey leggings. The small logo on the sweatshirt is written in white and says 'New Beginnings For Hurting Bodies.' Esther looks beautiful. I hate being here to eat more dirt from Alex McGrath. The mother of the baby and her friend are both overweight and they cycle slowly. The baby in the buggy twists the dummy around his mouth again.

'I wouldn't care if he did that all day,' says Esther.

Alex McGrath scratches his bald head. He is tall and wide and looks even more frightening than when he is surrounded by steam. He has aged better than some telegraph poles. His dark blonde hair at the side of his head is cut short like always. He wears a T-shirt that reads 'Adbury supports the countryside'. He smiles at the fat baby. On his arm, there is a tattoo that says 'Adbury born and bred'. The baby spins the dummy around his mouth and slaps his tiny thighs with his hands. The baby makes a baby noise. The two women on the exercise bikes pedal away. Esther rocks the buggy.

'Bring the kid to my place, Esther,' says Alex McGrath. 'I'll throw him in the pool.'

Esther looks at me but I say nothing. Elsewhere, a huge barrel-chested bloke lays on his back and lifts piled weights off his well developed chest. He shouts a strange noise. Close to the bloke with the big chest a woman with a headband and overgrown curly hair tramps a noisy treadmill. Exciting and challenging police work, this is not.

The pedalling mother checks to see if her child still exists. The baby turns his dummy around his mouth while he scratches his corduroy trousers.

'Don't say that's impressive,' says Alex McGrath.

'I bet you can't do it,' says Esther.

'It was rubbish the first time. Take my advice. This place needs more business, Esther.'

'The place looks good, nice and clean, no mess. I do all right for a woman on my own.'

Esther takes her hand off the buggy.

The movement is minimal but it reminds me of her physical

perfection. I should call her any angle Esther. The two girls working for Esther clean unused equipment. The two girls wear black latex tights and purple vests. The outfits show definite cleavage. The girls have impressive figures but neither is beautiful like Esther.

'I asked Nathan to be here,' says Alex McGrath. 'I want him to tell you in front of me that I have nothing to do with the terrible thing that happened to you. Well, Nathan.'

'I need to make further enquiries,' I say.

'That isn't what I said.'

I rub the bruise. It is a desperate attempt at a plea for sympathy from Esther.

'Alex had nothing to do with the terrible thing that happened to you, Esther,' I say.

Esther grins but it is sarcastic and a grin I could do without. She shakes her head in disbelief and flicks the pedal on the bike so it spins. I anticipate what will be an almighty row later.

On their bikes the two women pedal with more effort. They glare at the speedometers between the handlebars. The barrel-chested bloke lying on his back shouts something strange again. His weights crash against the machine. The woman on the treadmill looks intelligent under the headband, well, compared with the other customers. Esther smiles at the fat baby. I do not want to be here.

'Esther, listen,' says Alex McGrath. 'I admire you. Dirty secrets or not, you deserve better than Nathan. I wouldn't wish him on anyone.'

I say nothing.

Alex McGrath continues, 'I respect independent businesswomen. Me, I belong to a conglomerate. I haven't a clue how much I've invested or whether I'm making a profit. I had to ask the accountant for his permission to buy the Mercedes. It's like being a big kid again. You must feel like a pioneer, Esther.'

'Nathan might be useless,' says Esther, 'but why should I put up with you coming here to gloat?'

'Esther, I don't want you picked on,' says McGrath.

I say nothing because I am aware that I am being talked about as if I was an insect. Ah, what the hell.

The two women on their exercise bikes smile at one another. Why they smile, I do not know.

'A woman on her own, Esther,' says McGrath. 'Believe me. There are beasts around.'

Esther rocks the baby a couple of times.

'It's you, Alex,' she says. 'I told the police it's not right.'

'I know,' says Alex McGrath. 'Nathan came to see me.'

'Alex was adamant in his denials,' I say.

Esther looks at me as if I am pathetic.

She talks to Alex McGrath, 'I'm going to make a complaint about the police?'

'What, complain about Nathan?' says Alex McGrath.

'Why not? He needs something to buck him up.'

Alex thinks this is funny. He leans back on the polished exercise bench and stretches his legs.

'I'm too old to go out splashing paint,' he says. 'You just imagine what I'd look like.'

Esther kicks again the pedal of the bicycle that she leans on. She lets the pedal spin around below her dangling foot.

'All Adbury talks about you, Esther,' says Alex McGrath. 'You must see the looks. Esther, you need a friend. Nathan is not even a friend to himself. Somebody needs to look after him but not an independent businesswoman.'

'I look after myself,' I say.

'Shut up, Nathan. I have a past myself but I'm Adbury born and bred.'

He does not point at the tattoo that names his birthplace. Such restraint offers relief of a sort. McGrath stops talking and stares at the baby.

'Look, Esther,' he says. 'That kid's listening to every word I say.'

Esther walks away from the exercise bike while the pedal is

still spinning. She sits on the polished exercise bench, sits a few feet away from McGrath. I do not like looking at them sitting close together, even if they hate one another. I suppose I trust no one, really.

'Alex, you have no right to be here,' says Esther.

The two women on their exercise bikes pedal more slowly than before but the bloke with the big chest persists in rattling his exercise machine. The woman on the treadmill looks like someone with ambition. The two girls working for Esther carry their dust cloths back into the office, which is in the corner of the gymnasium. McGrath stares at their bottoms until they disappear.

'I'm not standing for this Fred Karno competition, Esther,' says Alex McGrath. 'You know the money I've spent on Barrel Park.'

'You've just said you were a conglomerate,' says Esther.

'Adbury needs Barrel Park. It needs a proper High Street. Not this dump stuck in the middle. How are we ever going to get investment here?'

'I'm providing employment.'

'It's not me going round saying you're running a knocking shop. Christ, Esther, I've built a swimming pool big enough to get tired in. Our architect has won awards. Adbury needs an image. You, a veggie restaurant and a hippie record shop and we're all finished. We've already got a stupid cinema.'

'Your place is too fancy. I provide an alternative.'

'The police think this is a knocking shop.'

'The police think what you tell them.'

The two women on their exercise bikes stop pedalling. They both lean their heads over their handlebars. The pain in their faces is obvious. With their legs splayed open, their bodies look heavier and the deterioration is more noticeable. The bloke with the barrel chest shouts and grumbles at the same time and sounds like he is having a loud argument with himself.

I am counting the minutes until this is over.

The mother of the baby climbs off her bike and walks over to the child. She takes the dummy out of the mouth and rubs it in the fat face, touches where the eyebrows should have been. The baby laughs and gurgles.

'The poor thing's missed his Mum,' says Esther, loud enough for the mother to hear.

I am not sure which is the worse torture, the intimidation of Alex McGrath or Esther talking like an idiot. The mother sucks the dummy. She has freckles all over her arms and dull grey eyes but she knows how to clean a dummy. The baby is happy with the cleaned dummy.

'He's been awfully good,' says Esther.

'I still have to have a shower,' says the mother.

'You're entitled to a shower. I'll shout if he gets restless.'

The mother tickles the baby under the chin. She smiles as the dummy goes around the mouth of her son a couple of times.

'You'll be fine, won't you, Cheeky?' she says.

The baby looks at least all right.

'The kid is addicted to the dummy,' says McGrath.

The mother towels her sweaty face.

'He'll soon have other interests besides dummies,' she says.

The mother and her friend walk towards the shower. They say hello to the barrel bloke as they pass by. The bloke with the big chest booms out a big grunt. The woman on the treadmill grins without altering her stride. Esther rocks the baby buggy to prevent the child missing his mother. The lower lip initially trembles but recovers. Esther stands up from the polished exercise bench and pushes the child and the buggy to the window. She stands next to me and talks quietly out the side of her mouth and into my ear.

'I fucking hate you,' she says.

Even close, she is unimpressed by the bruise.

'I'm going to make a complaint.' She speaks more loudly so Alex McGrath can hear. 'I will make allegations about you both.'

'I did what you asked, Esther,' I say.

Well, not really, I think.

McGrath drags himself over to the window. The barrel-chested bloke is still grunting. The woman on the treadmill remains preoccupied. I turn and stare down at the High Street to avoid looking at McGrath. The baby points at the people or something below. Because of the rain, many in the street below walk under umbrellas. A lonely damp pigeon flies from umbrella to umbrella.

'Don't make me worry about you, Esther,' says Alex McGrath. 'Realise I've always tried to be friendly.'

Esther surveys the street below.

'Work for me, Esther,' says Alex McGrath. 'You'd have a good salary.'

'Alex, I can pay wages myself,' says Esther.

'Nobody in Adbury really thinks New Beginnings is a knocking shop,' I say.

I am ignored.

'I got planning permission for New Beginnings,' says Esther. 'All on my own.'

Esther, McGrath and me look down at the High Street. Umbrellas below push the bare headed out of the way. We watch young people walk in and around the shoppers. The young people rattle tins and collect money. A huge temporary sign is hung over the entrance to The Little Picture House. The sign says, 'Oscar's Collection Fund. For our cinema.' The young people collecting money wear blue anoraks with the words 'LITTLE PICTURE HOUSE' written on the back.

'Another charity I'm obliged to give to,' says McGrath.

'It's good,' I say. 'Young kids collecting for our cinema.'

'Shut up, Nathan,' says Alex McGrath.

He faces Esther as if to explain.

'I couldn't entertain a film these days,' he says.

'I never feel right saying no to charities,' says Esther. "I'm a sucker for the *Big Issue* people.'

'Look, the baby is asleep,' I say.

The sleeping baby inspires a smile by McGrath.

'We'd make a good team, Esther,' he says. 'I could give you a living. I've never said anything to the police. I know you have a past, of course. I have instincts. I like your ideas.'

'I provide free MP3 players for the treadmills,' says Esther.

On the street below, I see Dr Long. She is my psychiatrist and has been for the last seven years, from when I was kidnapped and people thought I was dead. I see her once a fortnight and talk. So does Esther. I visit because Carl and others think I am crazy and because the Police Federation is willing to pay. Esther wants help with a problem I tell her is trivial. She is unable to hear her own voice for a sustained period. A couple of words and she thinks she sounds like someone else. She does not, and I know because I have to listen to her, but that is what she thinks. It worries her.

'I've written to the Chief Constable,' says Esther in the familiar and predictable voice. 'He's bringing in a Detective Superintendent from Liverpool. A woman. I made sure she knew you splattered paint all over my house.'

'To investigate Nathan,' says McGrath.

He is grinning at me.

'To investigate all of you,' says Esther.

Outside, the day has turned dark, and the rain is now much heavier. Esther watches the rain drop heavily on the umbrellas that hide the heads of the shoppers below. One umbrella drops forward until a full face is revealed. The woman with the face holds the open umbrella in front of her waist, points it at the pavement. The woman stands still and looks up at Esther. Rain falls down on her face and inside the upturned umbrella.

'Something wrong, Esther?' says McGrath.

Esther leaves her mouth open.

'Close your mouth, Esther,' says Alex McGrath.

'What?' she says.

'Blink or close your mouth.'

'She's staring at me.'

'How?'

'She's looking up at the window.'

The woman holds on to her umbrella and smiles at Esther. She makes no attempt to close the umbrella. The other shoppers have to walk around her. Her rain sodden hair makes the woman look younger. In the rain, her spiky hair looks indestructible.

'Who is she,' says Alex McGrath. 'Esther, do you recognise the woman.'

Esther looks pale and unhappy, frightened. I feel anxious about her which is a first that morning because up until then I have been anxious only about me.

'She's shouting something,' I say. 'She's soaked. She shouldn't be standing in the rain. She isn't all there.'

The woman stops shouting and smiles again. She freezes her smile, raises a finger and points it at Esther. She ignores the rain.

'This is getting embarrassing,' says Alex McGrath.

'Alex, please,' I say.

We all watch the woman finally close the umbrella and wink. Before the woman mouths the word goodbye, she turns and walks away. She laughs and shakes rain from her head at the same time. The other umbrellas move to let her pass.

'She was staring at me,' says Esther. 'She was laughing at me. Where on earth do you find these people? It's Nathan. You sent him to Leeds to find her. I shouldn't have to put up with this. You poking your nose everywhere.'

'The woman is a stranger to me,' says Alex McGrath. 'You've seen others? Tell me.'

'You put her up to this. God, you're crude.'

'Don't tell me what I am, Esther.'

Esther recovers some composure. Her breathing settles, and she closes her mouth.

'You have a past, Esther,' says Alex McGrath. 'You have secrets.'

I am ashamed. A long time ago, I did go to Leeds when McGrath asked me, because I was a little curious myself about what Esther had done there and about what people had said. I had thought

I could fob off Alex McGrath with a couple of harmless bits of information. The appearance of the woman is nothing to do with me. Behind us the brute working the weights has come to a stop. I hear his breathing idle to a recovery. The brute climbs to his feet and takes slow heavy steps towards the changing rooms. Alex McGrath waits until the brute has disappeared.

'Alex, I don't have to see you here again,' says Esther.

'You look at my swimming pool soon,' says Alex McGrath.

'I wouldn't even have you as a customer.'

'Let me tell you. You'd have anyone.'

McGrath stares again at the shoppers below.

'Look at them,' he says, almost like Orson Welles in *The Third Man*, 'small damp people having to rely on cheap umbrellas. I'm amazed any of us have enough confidence to think of people as customers, that we trust them to that extent.'

He looks sideways in both directions at the long window that overlooks the High Street.

'Were the council told everybody could see in like this?' he says.

'Alex, the customers like it,' says Esther. 'If they didn't want to be noticed, they wouldn't grow muscles. Okay? The next time you visit, I will call the police.'

'I called the police here this time. I called Nathan.'

'Nathan,' she says and grins in that unpleasant way that makes me uncomfortable.

'Don't be frightened of me, Esther. I came to offer help. Remember, you're a long way from Leeds. Know your friends.'

'This is the threat I'm to remember?'

I look at my reflection and the bruise on the side of my face that I would rather not see. Esther rocks the baby buggy a couple of times. I remember the woman standing in the rain and the soaked face below the indestructible hair. I am anxious.

6

NATHAN AND ESTHER IN BED

I am lying in bed alongside Esther. I am an orgasm lighter or, if you are the type that likes to spread misery, one orgasm closer to death. I still have an erection. Esther lifts up the duvet and peeps.

'I really did miss you,' I say.

'As if,' says Esther, 'you missed it, that's all.'

'I cannot believe you said yes, after this morning.'

'I missed it, too, and you are here, so why waste it. I always feel better with semen inside me.'

This is not a compliment. Esther grins horribly, and the remark is as cold and as hurtful as she intends.

'I actually hate you,' she says.

In comparison, this sounds tame. Nevertheless, I lose the erection. Esther lights a cigarette with a lighter that she bought in Spain. We watch TV, and I flick through the channels until Esther grabs the remote from my hand.

'Leave it be,' she says. 'I don't think you've done or said one decent thing all day.'

I remember the visit to New Beginnings For Hurting Bodies. I remember what happened in bed.

'Not one thing in the whole day,' I say. 'What about before?'

'I pretended you were Brad Pitt.'

'He is not your type.'

'I realise that now,' she says.

Esther smokes her cigarette, we say nothing and endure *BBC News*.

Esther eventually stubs out her cigarette and says, 'I was

ashamed of you this morning.'

I say nothing because I am ashamed as well.

'Why can't you stand up to him?' she says.

I say nothing because I am too ashamed to speak.

'I stand up to him,' says Esther.

'You're a woman,' I say. 'He will not hurt you like he will me. I have known physical pain. It frightens me. I was once brave. '

'I doubt it.'

'Well, I was different from what I am now. Heroes do not have nightmares. Nightmares make you compromise.'

Esther leaves the bed and puts on a shiny blue dressing gown, which may or may not be silk. I have never asked and, if I were less timid, I probably would have. Esther sits down on the bed again.

'I know you're twisted and damaged, Nathan,' says Esther. 'You wouldn't bother with me if you were all right. I'm a sad case. Because you read books and sound clever, I think you're superior. Well, I used to.'

'Perhaps I should have gone to Spain instead of you and stayed there,' I say.

Esther says nothing and sulks.

'Perhaps I should leave you to concentrate on your business,' I say.

'I wouldn't stay in Adbury just for you,' says Esther.

'I know that,' I say.

I do not say that what she has just said does not make sense.

'It wouldn't bother you if I walked, would it?' she says.

There are certain questions that are best not answered.

'I wish I could stand up to McGrath,' I say, 'but he is tougher than me and he has more allies than me. What do you expect me to do?'

'You can make it official, Nathan, like I did,' says Esther.

'If I was a fully functioning policeman, I would do something about Alex McGrath. I'm not the one to sort it out. I have psychiatric treatment once a fortnight.'

'And so do I.'

'It's not the same. You don't have nightmares.'

'I don't know why I hear other people's voices come out of my mouth. It disturbs me.'

'I've tried to explain it to you.'

'Yes, you're quite an expert about me. Did you go to Leeds for McGrath?'

'No,' I lie.

The truth is complicated but no excuse.

'You don't believe me, do you?' I say. 'You can't forgive me for something that I didn't do which is why you made the official complaint about me.'

I do not think what I have just said is credible but it sounds good.

'I complained about the police in Adbury,' says Esther.

'I've seen the complaint,' I say. 'You say I did not investigate the vandalism to your house. We forget that I was the one who had the damned paint removed.'

'You made one phone call. I wanted you to think about McGrath and what he's done to you. I thought making a complaint might help us.'

'You were thinking about yourself. No wonder you see a psychiatrist. You are as crazy as I am.'

I pick up the cigarette packet, open the lid but put it back down without being tempted. The eyes of Esther harden and become smaller. She still looks beautiful.

'You don't need to smoke,' she says. 'Do you, Nathan?' She is not interested in me answering and continues quickly. 'If you don't smoke, you can't really have an addictive personality. I was in your motor, Nathan. I was looking for your map of Macclesfield.'

'I don't keep it in the car,' I say. 'I keep my maps with my other books.'

'I found your stack, Nathan. I found the tin. It was simple. Don't let anybody ever say you're not neat and tidy. Everything in the right place, just like your home. You obviously need order in some things.'

I say nothing. I am pleased that she thinks my home is tidy although she does not visit anymore. Esther was always very quiet in my home, maybe the books affect the voices that she thinks come out of her mouth.

'You lied to me, Nathan,' she says. 'You're always lying to me. You tell me I'm beautiful. I won't ever trust you again.'

'Even on my bad days,' I say, 'I think you're attractive.'

'I brought you a nice present back from Spain.'

The present is actually naff but I say nothing.

'You're a lying pig,' she says. 'I don't need this shit. You said you only started the drugs because of what that gang did.'

'Seven years ago, everybody thought I had died a hero. But I came back a wreck,' I say. 'That disappointed everyone including me. I'm not on the drugs anymore. I agreed with the Federation to being medically supervised and tested. If I take drugs, it is reported to my superior.'

'You've got a stack in your car.'

'I know. After McGrath thumped me and, I hate to remind you, after I was told I was being investigated, I felt low. Someone approached me from the past. It was a coincidence. I bought some smack.'

'With the idea of using it?'

'No, not really, it was a defiant gesture that meant nothing. I am good at those, Esther. I had no intention of using the stuff. I couldn't if I wanted to. Sometimes, having it there makes it easier to do without. You don't understand, do you?'

'Fucking right,' she says.

I sigh and pull the pillow towards me. This time I am not lying.

'Nathan, it was over seven years ago,' says Esther.

'I thought I made you happy,' I say.

'I am happy, well sort of, but I don't want you on drugs. I want a bloke who has a shoulder I can lean on. I want a proper boyfriend.'

'They told me who would be investigating your complaint,' I say.

'She's from Liverpool,' says Esther.

'She isn't really. She used to work in Adbury.'

'How do you mean?'

'She knows me. She knows me very well.'

Esther laughs and says, 'You always fall on your feet.'

'She isn't here to investigate me,' I say.

'How do you mean?'

'She is here to confirm my fall from grace. Kate Moreton is a professional policewoman with a strongly developed sense of integrity. She is arriving to sanctify my humiliation. Thank you, Esther.'

'How do you mean she knows you well?'

I say nothing. I am still holding the pillow.

'She likes handsome men, then,' says Esther.

'She thought that I was clever and had potential,' I say.

'Carl says you were the cleverest kid in the school.'

'We're all obliged to perish.'

'How do you mean?'

'I can't keep getting cleverer.'

'Alex tells you not to see me, and you stand and take it.'

'I'm here, aren't I?'

'Behind his back, you are. Nathan, I want you to go home. No, I don't want you to do anything stupid. If you feel like that, you'd better stay. But I would prefer that you go home.'

'No, I can go home.'

'Is Kate Moreton attractive?'

I say nothing.

'I asked you a question.'

'I used to think so.'

Esther smiles and says, 'We've both had our eye wiped, then.'

7

NATHAN IN HIS HOME

I am in my dining room. I am listening to music, reading and sometimes drinking whisky from a glass, which I think might qualify as a tumbler. The conversation I had with Esther was long and difficult, and the memory embarrasses me but I still am able to read.

I am indulging myself with my obsession. The dining room table is covered with paper. In one corner are books, another has blank paper on which I can make notes, in another are articles that I have previously printed from my PC, and in the remaining corner are notes that I have made in the past. In the middle of it all is a contact book that lists the other people who share this obsession. All of them are strange like me. At our meetings we take photographs. These are not photographs that I share.

In the beginning, which is a less than accurate reference to my kidnap and when I returned home from being treated in hospital, I found the obsession helped. It calmed nerves. Now it does not but I am still obsessed.

'It all started after the dope,' Carl had once said.

He does not like me talking about Buckland House. He wants me to return to being normal. The way he thinks I was before being kidnapped. I have explained to him more than once.

I usually say, 'It's a poignant tale. And being interested in something over a period of time makes it more interesting. I can't make my mind up, Carl. How much is truth and how much rumour. But at least it is me deciding.'

I often dream about what happened at Buckland House, mainly

in the morning when I return to sleep. I imagine I am there seventy years ago when the bomb dropped on their exclusive ball. I am amongst the almost dead bodies and crawling around under the rubble of Buckland House. I brush against fingertips reaching for each other and I find the decapitated head of Armstrong Taylor-Fielder lying somewhere in the rubble.

Sipping whisky, my mind drifts towards reality and the present. I anticipate the arrival of Kate Moreton in Adbury. She will see me and know that I am different, realise that I am a shell. To stop worrying about Kate, I pick up another book. I always think of the ghosts loitering around Buckland House as guardian angels. The family was wiped out by the one bomb, the whole aristocratic line. The *National Trust* now owns the house. I imagine aristocrats inside their bomb-mauled bodies, now obliged to guard over visiting social inferiors. I search my own papers and remember my last visit to Buckland House, me taking photographs of the ruins. For a while I have thought that, if we are virtuous, we will stay and become the guardian angel of someone, or if we die early like the Armstrong Taylor-Fielders and have not had time to be bad. I assume that these guardian angels that I have invented can see us. Kate was always a frustrated guardian angel for someone, before she went to Liverpool, before we finished seeing one another. The affair with Kate had held my marriage together. Once she left and after the kidnap happened, well, everything fell apart.

A photograph of the Taylor-Fielder children makes me think of my two daughters whom I never see, whom I never bump into accidentally. I meet so many people in Adbury without warning, yet I never meet my children that way. I drink more whisky and write a task list identical to the one I had already written five minutes before.

8

NATHAN ON THE DANCE FLOOR IN BARREL PARK HOTEL

I am not really on the dance floor. I do not dance. I am close. I am sitting next to Carl at a large oval table. The dance floor, which is unfinished, is behind our backs. We face a huge window that is at least thirty feet long and twelve feet high. Alex McGrath faces Carl and me.

'Nathan, don't keep doing that,' says Alex McGrath.

I am scratching the white tablecloth. Carl has his mobile on the table close by and switched to vibrate. Carl worries about his mother and likes to be permanently available. The huge window is being splashed with rain. A large brown Labrador sits on the soaked lawn. In the rain the dog is the colour of chocolate. Carl puts his gloves inside his peaked cap and he pushes it forward so it hides the mobile. If the damned dog would stop staring at me, I might feel sorry for it. Alex McGrath wears jeans and a T-shirt and smokes a cigar. The rain continues.

'That dog out there is getting drenched,' says Carl.

'I expect obedience,' says Alex McGrath.

The dog looks as if it has just left a washing machine. McGrath leaves the cigar in his mouth and lets it burn. He does not turn his head to look at the dog. Without realising, I stroke the tablecloth with the tips of my fingers.

'Nathan, don't do that,' says McGrath.

Carl puts his hand on mine.

Stop it,' he says.

I put my hand out of sight.

The T-shirt that McGrath wears advertises the *Adbury Salt Mine Museum*. He stares at the unfinished dance floor behind Carl and me. I do not look but remember the huge pieces of plywood that have been nailed to the stanchions across the floor.

'It must be disappointing, Alex,' says Carl.

'Thirty thousand this has already cost me,' says McGrath. 'Let me tell you. Builders make promises.'

'You shouldn't hand thirty grand over.'

'He'll suffer. I'll make sure of that.'

I take an apple out of my pocket. I have had no lunch. I hold the apple in front of my mouth.

'Nathan, what are you supposed to be doing?' says Alex McGrath.

'I'm going to eat an apple,' I say.

'I like an apple,' says Carl.

'I'm not the only one,' I say.

Outside, the damned dog is still staring at me.

'I hardly ever have an apple,' I say. 'I found this, so I felt obliged.'

I have actually stolen it from the hotel reception of Barrel Park.

'Nathan,' says Alex McGrath, 'put down the fucking apple.'

I put down the apple. The damned dog watches it all. Alex McGrath sighs. He is a big man and when he sighs you hear him.

'We've Tudor fronts,' says Alex McGrath 'The High Street should be an attractive feature.'

'They're not real Tudor houses,' says Carl.

'New shitty Beginnings and a daft picture house.'

'My Dracula week wasn't a success,' I say.

'Nathan, people don't like the black and whites,' says Carl. 'I only went to keep you happy.'

'You're as daft as him,' says McGrath. 'New Beginnings looks like a knocking shop.'

'Alex, this is beginning to sound like a record,' says Carl.

'This is not a zombie apocalypse.'

Or even a few vampires, I think. I pick up the apple again.

'If you fucking eat that,' says Alex McGrath.

Outside, the damned dog still stares at me. I put the apple back on the table. Alex McGrath balances his burning cigar on top of the apple.

'The girls in New Beginnings are most attractive,' I say.

I worry about his cigar burning a hole in my apple.

'They're not prostitutes,' says Carl. 'We know prostitutes.'

'Prostitutes always offer Carl sex,' I say.

'Everyone knows I'm a good payer,' says Carl.

He grins like a man who is not wearing a uniform. Before the uniform, he used to wear short sleeves in winter. Nobody ever expected Carl to become Superintendent. He looked different in short sleeves.

'Not that I would pay,' says Carl. 'I'd be too embarrassed.'

'Both of you get yourself nice girlfriends,' says McGrath. 'Don't bother with prostitutes, Carl.'

'I don't go to prostitutes. I'd feel silly. I'm all right. Women think I have a sense of humour.'

'Women will laugh at anything,' says Alex McGrath.

'They don't laugh at Nathan,' says Carl. 'They think he's too serious.'

'When you're old you can spot a genuine woman,' I say. 'I can smell nice girls.'

'The not so nice girls smell nicer,' says Carl.

'Esther is not a nice girl,' says Alex McGrath. 'I'm telling you.'

Carl and me look at each other. We acknowledge the shared burden of having to listen to Alex.

'I didn't paint her fucking house yellow,' says Alex McGrath.

'If I understood correctly,' I say, 'I was supposed to investigate the incident.'

'I'm talking to Carl. Don't interrupt, Nathan.'

'Esther was the victim of a crime, Alex.'

'The stupid cinema has enough space for three shops. Add on Esther and you've lost half the fucking street.'

'Hardly.'

'He's now a qualified surveyor.'

Alex McGrath picks up his cigar from my apple. He takes a drag and puts the cigar back on the apple. My apple is changing colour, to something similar to the damned dog that keeps staring at me.

'I've heard all about that picture house,' says Alex McGrath. 'There are nights they wait for customers before switching on the film.'

'That happened in my vampire week,' I say. 'It's famous, Alex. It's been in the *Guardian*. It's been showing Westerns since Sunday.'

'It's always fucking Westerns. They were all in here giving out leaflets.'

'*Stagecoach* tonight,' I say.

'Black and white films can't be good for Adbury. Christ, we're battling against global capitalism, Third World labour.'

'It showed musicals last week. Three Gene Kelly films, in fact.'

'Don't I know,' says Alex McGrath. 'I had the Gene Kelly fan club staying here.'

'Well, then,' I say.

Carl is not listening. He is only pretending. I know the look. His red face looks especially smooth when he is still.

'They commented on no dance floor,' says Alex McGrath.

'You wouldn't want everyone in here pretending to be Gene Kelly,' says Carl.

Sorry, Carl really was listening. The damned dog outside is definitely watching me.

'Thirty thousand for no dance floor,' says Alex McGrath.

'But no Gene Kellys,' I say.

'Shut up, Nathan.'

'There are Gene Kelly fans all over the place,' says Carl. 'My mother was a fan. Now, she wouldn't know Gene Kelly from Fred Astaire.'

'I think they should close the cinema down,' says Alex McGrath.

'Not before you get the dance floor,' I say.

Carl smiles.

The cigar is still on the apple and the cigar is still burning. The apple is now brown all over.

'My stock car racetrack has lost money for twelve months,' says Alex McGrath.

'God, it was always packed when we were kids,' says Carl. 'I had good times there.'

'The hot dog men are like gardeners. I tell you. You see them a couple of times and that's it. Never turn up again.'

'What more do you want, Alex? The hotel is fabulous.'

'I told you. I want to put Adbury on the map.'

Outside, the Labrador settles down to sleep in the damp grass.

'Forget that,' says Carl. 'Worry about what Esther will tell Kate when she arrives.'

'I thought it was a complaint about Nathan,' says Alex McGrath.

'Our Kate has a nose. If she starts digging.'

'The damage that woman Esther has done.'

'I always feel sorry for a woman on her own in a big house.'

'She isn't alone. Nathan pesters her.'

'I could never leave my mother all alone,' says Carl. He switches off the light on his mobile. 'My mother hated me being in the police. She thought I'd be on the beat for the rest of my life. For so long now, she's had to do what I've told her.'

McGrath picks up his cigar. The apple rolls a couple of inches towards me. Burnt, it is much reduced. Compared to the apple, the wet Labrador is lucky. McGrath takes a long drag of his cigar. Outside, the Labrador opens his eyes again. The rain does the inevitable, and the dog does his best to think it through. McGrath takes another drag.

'Smoking causes fatal diseases,' I say. 'So do attacks on women.'

'You can't help yourself, Nathan, can you?' says Alex McGrath.

'I thought I was offering advice.'

'It's a shame about the dance floor,' says Carl.

'I don't dance,' I say.

'I don't mind a dance. All we want, Alex, is for you to stay quiet. Take a breather. Leave Esther be. Certainly while Kate is in town.'

'Carl, don't come round here to give me a warning,' says Alex McGrath. 'Not even advice, you come here, you be polite.'

'Come on, we're still friends. We'll always do our best.'

'What about you, Nathan?'

'I'm not as reliable or as important as Carl,' I say. 'I would struggle to know what my best was now.'

'He has good days and bad days,' says Carl.

'Some days I don't give a fuck.'

'Shut up, Nathan,' says Alex McGrath.

Carl pulls his uniform jacket until it is neat and without creases.

'We've got to be above board, Alex,' he says.

McGrath stands up, turns his back on Carl and me and walks over to his window. He opens the giant window and steps outside. He throws the cigar at the Labrador and steps back inside out of the rain. The Labrador lets the cigar bounce off his head. McGrath sits down in the same place.

What the hell, I think.

'You two have been at this bar till well past midnight,' says Alex McGrath. 'Don't forget yourself, Superintendent.'

Carl sits up straight.

'And we've worked,' he says. 'A hint of trouble, and we've been here.'

'Barrel Park has one hundred per cent law enforcement,' I say. 'Drunks, vandals and deadbeats, you have no idea of the minor irritations other people have to put up with.'

'We've been pleased to help,' says Carl. 'Anyway we can. We don't want you upset. I don't like to see anyone upset.'

'You think I'm an arse wipe,' says McGrath.

'I don't think that necessarily follows,' I say.

'Nathan, spare us the analysis.' says Carl. 'Alex, I know this.

Esther Welles has written to the Chief Constable complaining about Nathan. At the moment, it's silly. But it has potential. Kate is only here for a few days. She is seeing old friends. I doubt if she'll work more than a day. Please keep things peaceful.'

The dog is disenchanted with the damp grass. He stands up and stares at me.

'You tell Esther she's out of order,' says Alex McGrath. 'This is a woman who's been fucked by all sorts, not just Nathan. Believe me.'

'I'm a Superintendent,' says Carl. 'I am not a blind company man but I have to promote equality, diversity and customer service. It's a system.'

Now Alex McGrath talks to me. 'What the fuck's he talking about?'

'I don't think we should mention Esther being fucked by anyone,' says Carl. 'Alex, Kate is a Detective Superintendent. She may be up for a trip to her old haunts but she is not going to be sloppy.'

'You two are wallowing in this. I can see. Nathan's to blame for this.'

Carl picks up my apple from the table. Carl is not known for being thoughtful but he looks at the apple as if it is a mystery. Isaac Newton, of course, started with an apple.

'I have two great qualities,' says Carl. 'I can take orders and I can look the other way when needed. It is why I am a successful policeman.'

It certainly is not brains, I think.

'Alex, we're a small town,' says Carl. 'We're all easy to turn over. This could be a riot without the laughs.'

'I've donated money to your charities,' says Alex McGrath. 'I've sponsored your football team.'

'I don't underestimate Kate,' says Carl.

He keeps hold of my apple.

'I think we should go,' I say.

Carl and me stand up at the same time. The Labrador barks.

'You're not always easy, Alex,' says Carl.

He smiles. Carl hardly ever speaks without smiling. Much of it means little. Carl impresses no one but somehow he keeps control.

'Look, boys,' says Alex McGrath. 'Get yourself a drink. I'll bring the dog in. We've worked well together.'

'The town has benefitted,' says Carl.

He picks up his peaked cap and gloves. He gives the apple back to me. He pockets his mobile phone.

'We're being friendly,' says Carl. 'We'd hoped you'd understand.'

'I didn't paint that house yellow,' says McGrath.

9

NATHAN IN ANOTHER
RESIDENTIAL HOTEL

I am in a room in this cheap scruffy hotel. I am lying on the bed with a pillow over my head. The gesture, rather than the pillow, is meant to mitigate pain.

I hear knocking at the door.

'Nathan, Nathan, open the sodding door.'

Carl kicks the door. He kicks it again, this time harder. The rest of the hotel is quiet and empty. Everywhere in the hotel is untidy and dirty, not just the bedrooms. The receptionist, who is called Vanessa, looks worse than the hotel. Even the immigrants, who are obliged to stay here, complain.

'You all right in there?' says Carl.

I do not answer. I keep the pillow over my head.

'You comfortable in there?' says Carl.

This is not an easy question to answer, I think.

Carl kicks the bottom of the door again.

'Nathan, I'm not going to go,' says Carl. 'Nathan, I'm wasting a life out here.'

He bangs the door a couple of times. I think he is using his fist. I take the pillow away from my head. I somehow stand and walk along the scruffy bedroom wall to the door. The room is full of rubbish, and not all of the wallpaper has remained on the walls. I accidentally kick an empty whisky bottle, and it rolls ahead of me, leads the way to the door.

I open the door.

'Nathan, this is out of order,' says Carl.

I blink a couple of times and burp. This causes me to fall over.

'I'm past caring, Nathan,' says Carl.

He looks down at my slumped body at his feet. I groan because I feel terrible.

'Don't ask me to pick you up,' says Carl.

I lift myself and climb the wall in stages. I prop myself against the doorframe. I close my eyes. Something flicks the end of my nose. I open my eyes.

'Who is it hitting the end of my nose?'

'Me,' says Carl. 'I should take a photograph. Have a laugh.'

I stare below my sick stomach at my bare feet and moan again. I do different things. I pull up my jeans until they meet my shirt. I scratch my neck and stroke the stubble on my face.

Carl says nothing.

'I am not at my best,' I say.

'What's caused this?'

'I can't face Kate.'

'It's trivial.'

'Esther will tell her everything.'

'About McGrath?'

'About me.'

I stare at the whisky bottle at my feet. I put a foot over the label, as if hiding temptation. Carl turns me around so I face the bedroom and he pushes me inside. I allude to incomprehensible agony but manage to stagger forward. The short corridor inside the bedroom is narrow, and I brush against walls. I fall face down on the bed and bury my head in the pillow again.

I hear Carl say, 'Don't do that, Nathan, you look like a child.'

I mumble something into the pillow that even I am unable to hear. I feel Carl sit down on the edge of the bed. I take the pillow from my head and open my eyes. The half wallpapered walls match the basic furniture. The TV is missing from the bracket on the wall. The sheets on the bed are old and thin but clean. They are as white as hospital bandages.

'Come on, Nathan,' says Carl. 'Let's get you comfortable.'

Carl adjusts the pillows and turns me around. I sit up.

'This place is for people on Social Security with nowhere to live,' says Carl. 'Nathan, we pay for a psychiatrist to avoid all this upset.'

I pick up my *Guardian* newspaper from the floor. I turn the pages quickly before abandoning it. I hold my head because it aches.

'I have been brooding for some time,' I say.

'Nathan, we support you. I let you have sick leave. Dr Long will give you a sick note anytime. But we can't have you turning up for work and going on the booze. This compromises me, Nathan. If Dr Long isn't helping, we'll get someone else.'

'Whatever her faults, I like my psychiatrist.'

'We have to meet Kate this afternoon.'

'I don't want Kate to know that I'm seeing a psychiatrist.'

'Sorry but she will,' says Carl. 'You had to get involved with Esther.'

'I do hate McGrath. I am abandoning the booze, Carl.'

'I know you are.'

Carl tries to make himself comfortable at the bottom of the bed.

'I imagined I would really enjoy the whisky,' I say.

'We're all fighting losing battles, Nathan,' says Carl. 'My mother called the police last night. She thought she had a burglar sitting on the sofa. Damn, this bed is uncomfortable.'

He stares out of the tiny window. I have done it myself, looked down on the roof of the railway station and thought of successful people rushing to catch trains. I am curious about whether Kate has travelled down by train. Carl rests his red face in his white hands. The effect is odd, I think. I realise that Carl is not wearing his uniform. These days he looks like a Superintendent all the time. I raise myself and sit with my back against the headrest. I lift up my right foot and let it rest on my left knee. I pull dried skin off my big toe.

'I am no use to anyone like this,' I say. 'Esther will talk to Kate about McGrath.'

'We have a peaceful town,' says Carl. 'People come to live here because it's safe. Neither you nor me have taken a penny off McGrath.'

'He is a criminal, Carl.'

'I call it proportionate policing. I know what to say to Kate. You're not going to mess up, Nathan. You're going to get yourself sober and be ready for Kate. We'll first go home, and I'll get my uniform.'

'I would hate to create a mess.'

I smile to show I have decent instincts.

'You have to have that first drink, Nathan,' says Carl.

'Kate has done well in Liverpool,' I say.

'You've got to freshen up,' says Carl. 'You've got a bit to do. You look terrible when you're not clean.'

'Lift me off the bed please.'

'I want you to make the effort.'

Carl walks into the bathroom. I listen to him run the shower. Carl stays in the bathroom. I listen to a train leave the station outside. The noise of the train drowns out the noise of the shower. My thoughts drift. I picture Carl in a different room, sitting behind a desk and facing an interviewing panel of two men and a woman. I think about Carl and the ease with which he probably convinced them. My head still aches. Carl appears and tells me to go and wash.

10

NATHAN IN THE CANTEEN

I am sitting with Carl in an alcove at the back of the police canteen. The other tables are empty, I think. We cannot see anyone else, which is why we decided to sit in the alcove. I can hear, though, Doreen, the canteen manager, working in the kitchen. She is a noisy worker, which I like. I have drunk a lot of coffee and breathed plenty of fresh air. Occasionally I also hear people come and buy something from the drinks and chocolate machine. Two pain-killing tablets after seeing Carl, I still have a headache but I am being sensible. I have to see Kate at four this afternoon, and it is past two. I am heavy with dread but I have no choice. I am drinking bottled water because I cannot drink any more coffee. I am now smartly dressed, and Carl is wearing his uniform.

'Cheer up, Nathan,' says Carl. 'We can get by. Who needs glory, I say. How about some spooky jokes, Nathan?'

'What, vampire jokes?' I say.

'Something to make us laugh, Nathan.'

'I think I would need a build up.'

'What I'd like, Nathan, are your powers of recovery. You don't look the same man.'

I say nothing and make no noise.

'I know something that will amuse you,' says Carl.

'I didn't ask, Carl.'

'Let me have a drink first.'

Carl finishes his cup of tea.

'I once picked up this piece,' he says.

This tale I have heard, I think.

'No more than eighteen she was,' says Carl, 'and thick as two short planks.'

'I didn't ask, Carl.'

'I know but you're curious. We were both young. Both of us were just out of the local comp'. We'd have been as daft if we'd been sober.'

I have worked with Carl for twenty years, and there are times when we have had to stand side by side. But he is not a man I know. He is a colleague.

'We went back to this pokey flat that belonged to a mate of mine,' says Carl. 'I'm still standing but it isn't. You know what I mean, Nathan? Well, she is hungry, and I recover. I don't feel so bad anymore. It's Saturday night. She's not messing.'

I know that Carl lives with his mother and has had girl friends but never left home. He is not hard working but knows how to cover his back. Nothing about police work impresses him but he is regarded as loyal.

'She was dead keen,' says Carl. 'Didn't even block my hands as they moved around.' Carl laughs. 'It wasn't my hands she was interested in. She was a little devil really. Christ, I was rampant. Whooh. Gets hold of my prick without me asking. It's too good to be true. Oh. Oh, indeed. Time of the month.'

'That doesn't matter,' I say.

'Long as you remember to put it behind your ear.' Carl laughs loudly. 'There's no reason for it to interfere with anybody's satisfaction.'

Carl is a man who talks a lot but I cannot say what interests him. He watches things like football, TV and films but rarely mentions what he has seen, merely that he watches. I am not sure how he talks so much. He talks about work, of course, but even that he keeps simple and brief.

'I doubt if people today would be as daft. Me and you, Nathan, are from the dark ages.'

He does talk about sex more than most, I suppose. Nobody thinks he is serious, though.

'I was only eighteen but I'd read about it all right,' says Carl. 'I knew about there being nothing wrong with the time of the month. It used to be in different magazines. What I hadn't read was that you had to take the tampon out first.'

Carl stops to take a breath.

I do not know what makes Carl anxious or indeed if he ever is.

'Oh, yes,' says Carl. 'I do not jest.'

I say nothing and think about a man whom I do not understand and him helping me in the hotel that morning.

'Didn't occur to her, either,' says Carl. 'To be fair, she had been drinking. I suppose you're bound to forget it after a while. If it's there between your legs.'

'I don't think I would,' I say. 'She must have been really drinking, Carl.'

'You'd have thought she'd have said when I was doing the business, back and forth so to speak. Up and down. Pushing it deeper inside her all the time. But? Maybe? Who knows? I can be gentle and loving.'

This is hilarious, not funny just hilarious.

'I had had a few pints, though.'

'You were probably quick,' I say.

'I'm never quick after a pint. We did it three times. I'd have done it more except the mate in the bedroom moaned about the noise.'

'I can imagine you making a lot of noise,' I say.

I cannot, I find it impossible to imagine him filling a life with anything. He is a colleague, a pretend person.

'Christ, when you're young,' says Carl. 'She was an uninhibited girl. At least, she enjoyed her pleasure.' Carl laughs. 'The older you get the better you were.'

'Wasn't she sore?'

'She didn't say so. I don't think she was. I'm kissing the top of her head dead romantic, swallowing her dandruff. The mate gets moaning again, so I decide its time we get a move on. I tell her to do the same. I'm struggling with my pants, thinking I'm doing all right considering. Thinking, in fact, it can't get any better than this. I was eighteen. The bit of stuff speaks to me.'

'Carl,' I say, 'you shouldn't call a woman a bit of stuff.'

I realise that I do not know what Carl wants for the future or if he has any plans. He has plans in work but they are imposed. We only talk about what we have to do and what others want. What he wants is beyond me.

Carl continues, 'The girl says, 'Carl', my name and nothing else and not very loud but I can tell from her face she's something on her mind.'

Of course, it is not just Carl whom I struggle to describe. The other policemen and policewomen are the same. I can describe Esther if I have to. I know what hurts her and what she wants.

'I notice this thin white string hanging down just a little bit between her legs,' says Carl. 'She's not happy. She's not bowlegged but she's not happy.'

'This is horrible,' I say.

'She bends her knees so there's a gap between her legs. She pulls on the string. Nothing happens. I can picture her now. Pulling on this string, looking at me. Not critical, just desperate for help. Dead trusting. Even standing strange, she had a great body. I had to do something, didn't I? I'm still full of ale, of course. You know what it's like. Makes you dead decisive.'

I was the same with Kate, knew what she wanted and what hurt but also more, what inspired her. As hard as I try, I cannot imagine Carl being inspired.

'I walked up close,' says Carl. 'I smiled to reassure her. I put my hand between her legs. Before she can ask, I grab hold of the little bit of string and pull down as hard as I could.'

Carl giggles and laughs. His red face is wide-eyed and smiling.

'She did more than blink, I can tell you. But she didn't cry. Honest, Nathan, her eyes had real shock. Afterwards, her legs trembled against my hand. They were so cold they gave me a fright. You know what sticks in my mind? Haunts me really.

The tampon. It whistled as it came out of her. It made a noise. Dead loud and high pitched like cats do in the night. But she was all right. That bloody whistle, I thought I'd done her damage, Nathan. I took her home to her Mum and Dad. If I remember right, we even walked home. I think she was grateful for the company. She's married now and not without cash. Even though she's got money, I can still hear that damned string whistle.'

I hear a chair being moved. It does not sound like Doreen in the kitchen. A woman appears at the head of the alcove. It is Kate. She is as I remember, tall, elegant, sharp eyed and clean. The six years have not changed her.

'Kate,' says Carl. 'We're having a late lunch.'

Kate ignores Carl and speaks to me.

'I'm disgusted with you, Nathan.'

Carl once described Kate as just another airhead with ambition. But he does not know her, does not know what she wants and what makes her feel hurt. She stands straight and looks down her nose all the way to me. I am embarrassed and ashamed but her appearance also makes me feel pain from before today, pain that I never quite forget.

'We've just been talking pleasantly over a cup of tea,' says Carl.

'Very loudly,' says Kate.

Carl stops grinning. Kate folds her arms.

'Remember, children,' she says. 'Nathan, I'm talking to you. Could you lift your head?'

I do as she says.

'I'm here because I have to be,' says Kate. 'I'm not obliged to be offended by small minded slobs waiting to grow up.'

The red face of Carl looks warm.

'The last thing you two need is another complaint,' says Kate.

'We were unwinding,' says Carl. 'Taking a breather. Nathan is an old friend. We've both been in the dumps. I had no idea you were listening. I don't want to upset you, Kate.'

I stand up. I stare into the green eyes of Kate. I want to say that

I am really sorry. Instead, I try to be clever.

'Back among the blackberry pickers, Kate,' I say. 'It's a poem by Seamus Heaney.'

'I'll look out for it,' she says.

She is wearing a grey suit and a white shirt. Her hair is quite short. I always found it easy to remember her outfits and hairstyles. This is another picture to add to the collection in my memory.

'You should be ashamed of yourself, Nathan,' says Kate.

'I am,' I say, 'every day.'

11

NATHAN IN INTERVIEW ROOM 3 ADBURY POLICE STATION

I sit opposite Kate on the other side of a small square table. The room is also square. The walls are plain, and the door is closed. Kate puts a bulky cassette into the tape machine.

This is the interview that occurred. This is what is on the tape. Wheedle your way into Adbury police station and you might hear it.

Kate: Detective Superintendent Kate Moreton, Interview with Detective Sergeant Nathan Wrench. Time, 16.05. Present – Kate Moreton and Nathan Wrench.

Pause.

Kate: Hello, Nathan. First, can you confirm that you have been advised that you can have a representative in attendance?

Me: Yes.

Kate: You want this interview to proceed without a representative?

Me: Yes.

Kate: You are aware that there has been a complaint about you from Esther Welles?

Me: Yes.

Kate: Do you understand the nature of that complaint?

Me: Yes.

Kate: Esther Wells says that she called the police to investigate the damage that was done to her property and that you failed to investigate properly. Is that what you understand?

Me: Yes.

Kate: Can you tell me what happened exactly?

Me: Yes

Kate: Will you?

Me: Yes.

Kate: If you would then.

Me: It is in the report. I visited after she called me to say that the house had been vandalised. I asked questions. She told me that she had just returned from a holiday in Spain but I knew that anyway. She asked me to make enquiries, talk to the neighbours and so on. She also asked me to talk to Alex McGrath. The incident was complicated by two factors.

Kate: What were they?

Me: I have a relationship with Esther Welles.

Kate: You live together?

Me: No. I visit her at her home. She does not visit me at mine. We do what people do in relationships. So my first conversation with Esther Welles was not typical of a police enquiry. I asked for details about the incident but I also asked Esther Welles whether she had enjoyed her holiday. The second complicating factor was that this incident occurred when Esther Welles was on holiday.

Kate: You do not have to keep calling her Esther Welles.

Me: Yes. The incident had occurred three days earlier and had already been investigated by a patrol officer. I referred back to her after my visit to Esther. She confirmed that the house had been painted yellow by three men who had arrived in a white van. The van had the name of a company on the side, and the three men wore overalls. The neighbours may have thought it strange that Esther wanted to paint her house yellow but nobody approached the three men. Some neighbours, though, did take details. They phoned the police. The patrol officer arrived after the three men had left in their van. I presume that if the neighbours had come out, the three men might have stopped and disappeared in the white van. The patrol officer, who wrote the report before I arrived at the scene of the crime, checked the details of the van and the company.

The registration number and the name of the company were both false. There was no telephone number on the side of the van. The patrol officer also interviewed the neighbours and collected witness reports. They are in her report but also duplicated in mine for completeness.

Kate: So did you do anything other than read her report?

Me: Yes. I annotated her report and made suggestions to the patrol officer for further action. Two reports are attached to my report, the original from the patrol officer and the same report with my annotations. I also contacted Environmental Health to remove the paint.

Kate: Had this not been done previously by the patrol officer?

Me: No, the patrol officer is a new recruit. She has noted the procedure for the future.

Kate: Was that it?

Me: No.

Kate: What else did you do?

Me: Esther believed that the incident was caused by Alex McGrath. They both own a gymnasium, and conflict exists between Esther and McGrath. I spoke to McGrath and asked him if he was involved in the incident, and he denied it. Neither the patrol officer nor me obtained evidence of McGrath being involved. The patrol officer made enquiries, and so did I. Both are documented in the reports. The patrol officer made official approaches to employees of McGrath. I approached known sources of information and made discreet observations. They are recorded in the report. There is nothing to link Alex McGrath to the incident.

Kate: Why do you think Esther Welles was unhappy with your investigation?

Me: I have no idea.

Kate: Did you tell Esther Welles the outcome of the investigation?

Me: I did but I also asked the patrol officer to visit and provide a full account of the joint enquiry. Later, I confirmed that the visit did take place.

Kate: Can I ask you a personal question?

Me: Yes.

Kate: You mention that you and Esther Welles have a personal relationship?

Me: Yes.

Kate: Do you argue?

Me: Everybody does.

Kate: Do you think Esther Welles has a grievance against you?

Me: No.

Kate: So why would she complain?

Me: Esther believes that Alex McGrath is engaged in criminal activity and that the police ignore it.

Kate: And do they?

Me: No.

Kate: Esther Welles has alleged that you went to Leeds on behalf of Alex McGrath to investigate what she did there.

Me: No, not on behalf of Alex McGrath. My Superintendent asked me to visit. He had received an allegation that Esther Welles was using an alias and that she was the subject of a police investigation.

Kate: Is she using an alias?

Me: Yes

Kate: Why would she do that?

Me: She wants to break with the past. She had a difficult time when she was young.

Kate: She used to be a prostitute?

Me: Yes

Kate: Were you in the relationship with Esther Welles at the time of your enquiries in Leeds?

Me: No.

Kate: Is Alex McGrath a paid police informer?

Me: No.

Kate: Have you ever obtained evidence of criminal activity against Alex McGrath?

Me: No.

Kate: Have you investigated other allegations of his criminal activities?

Me: Yes and I have arrested people who may have worked for him. But if they do, they are incredibly loyal. He is a rich businessman. If he is a criminal, he pays others. Those we arrest do not incriminate him.

Kate: Have you ever considered a plan to entrap Alex McGrath?

Me: No

Kate: Why not?

Me: That policy would have to be decided by a superior.

Kate: I do not have any more questions. Is there anything that you would like to add?

Me: No.

Kate: Thank you Detective Sergeant.

Me: Thank you Detective Superintendent.

And that is it. My brain recalls the questions as I watch Kate switch off the recording machine. She was, as I expected, professional. Apart from the odd moment of perjury, I think I did okay.

12

KATE RUNS IN CHESHIRE

There were no metal men here, no breeze from the sea, no waves lapping against the beach. Kate was alone in front of the entrance to her hotel. She rested one foot on the bottom doorstep. The car park was illuminated with over-powered lights. The tarmac was somehow bright grey. Kate bent her knees to loosen her hamstrings. She checked her watch, counted down the seconds. The actual time was fifteen minutes past seven.

Kate ran through the car park, happy to run under bright lights and to pass stationary cars. A narrow lane of bulky stones and pebbles led the way out of the car park. Kate ran between two rows of tall hedges. Her trainers splashed through various puddles. The beams from the lights in the car park soon faded, and the lane became dark. The lane sloped uphill, and her breathing quickened, and Kate experienced the usual doubts before she found her second wind. Her eyes adjusted to the dark a little, and she relaxed. Kate felt defiant and strong.

The lane opened out into a narrow road where she ran along flat tarmac and splashed through less frequent puddles. Trees replaced the hedges. A car overtook her before she heard it properly. The car passed by more closely than she would have liked but she appreciated the brief spell of light from the headlamps. She managed to follow the red lights for a few extra seconds. After that, Kate followed the road and kept close to the grass bank at the edge of the tarmac.

Kate thought of her ex-husband and the few occasions they had attempted to run together. The darkness around the narrow road helped her think of him dead and his pathetic lost spirit floating away from them all. She listened to her trainers slap against the tarmac.

There was enough light from the moon for Kate to see the outline of the trees and clouds. In the dark the trees appeared malformed and crippled, ready to unleash resentful taunts. The clouds above were heavy and anxious, clearly critical. Kate told herself to stop thinking. She put her hands into the pockets of her shorts, comforted herself by feeling the stopwatch and pocket panic alarm. She heard a stream run alongside the road. The noise of persistent running water helped her imagine the fields and trees in normal daylight. She remembered waves lapping against a beach.

Kate took her hands out of her pockets. She flattened her hair with her hands. She wiped the sweat off her hands on to her sweater. A car appeared ahead, dazzled her and passed by before she had time to shield her eyes. Kate ran past more trees, appreciated them all looking different from each other. She ran up another hill, pleased to have to make an effort again and realising that without physical diversions she was capable of creating imaginary terror if the mood took her.

Just don't, she said.

Kate ran along more flat ground. Once or twice, by mistake, she stepped into the grass bank at the side of the road. The trees and fields had changed into a different shade of grey. The moon above was smaller. Kate realised she was running against the wind. The air turned cold and unfriendly. Kate remembered from her childhood how she would create the idea of someone close behind and breathing over her, someone who would not go away.

This is daft, she said to herself, just stop it.

The flat road came up against a fence and more trees. Kate turned left into a lane narrower than the previous road. The lane had passing spaces for cars, and Kate ran into them for the extra exercise. She no longer heard any noise from the river but the wind against her face was less unfriendly. She recalled her childish notion and remembered how quickly it would become a fixation. All it ever required was the feeling of being alone. To give her something different to do, she listened to her breathing. It sounded healthy enough. Despite the *aches in her stomach that had plagued her for the last two months, she was not even nauseous. The wind passed across her shoulder blades. Kate could not help imagining fingers stroking her spine, a vague creature with long arms stretching out across fields to touch her, sharp fingernails leaving pinpricks of ice in the middle of her back. Kate ran past the next passing space without being tempted to run inside. She turned her head around to check there was no one behind and saw nothing but darkness and the trees. Kate laughed at herself for being stupid but she was pleased she had been able to look behind.*

This is really stupid, she said.

All I have to do is prove that I possess more nerve than a child does. She imagined a creature so quick it could move out of sight every time she turned her head.

For Christ sake, she said.

In defiance, Kate ran twice around the next passing space.

She imagined a creature that could run with exactly the same footsteps as her own.

Kate took the panic alarm out of her pocket, clutched it tight inside her palm.

This is perverse, she said.

Kate found the next left turn. The lane widened again, and the passing spaces disappeared. She kept to the gravel at the edge of the road so she could hear some noise. The clouds around the moon parted slightly, took a hesitant breath. The extra moonlight, the noise of the gravel and the wider lane all helped. Kate put the panic alarm back in her pocket. She ran up another hill, avoided looking at the trees in the fields in case they were pointing at a creature behind her back.

You'll be able to see your way round all right, Carl had said.

The man was an idiot.

Running up the next hill tired Kate enough for her to forget the creature behind her. When she was back on flat ground, she concentrated on maintaining the same level of effort. She tried to imagine the creature again but failed. She heard herself chuckle.

This is better than anything, she thought. Breathing with your lungs pumped open. Not an ache or pain in your body anywhere. Her age a heroic bonus and not a burden.

Kate noticed the light arrive around her feet and seep sideways across the lane. She looked quickly over her shoulder. The headlights on the car behind were on full beam. She deliberately made an effort not to slow down, counted down a minute before looking at her feet again. The light around her feet was still there. The car was travelling at the same speed as Kate ran.

She took out the panic alarm again, almost fumbled it into a hedge. Her fingers found the red button. She remembered the car that had passed by earlier in the other direction and feared it might have turned round to follow her. The beam from the headlights ended a few inches in front of her feet. Unable to escape the beam, Kate felt as if she was running on the spot. The trees at the side of the lane no longer looked threatening, just stupid and useless. Kate realised her breathing was different from before. She looked behind again. The headlights were big, bright and solid white.

Kate nearly missed her next turn and would have done if there had not been the bright lights from the hotel car park shining over the top of the final hill. In the half-dark the lit hotel was full of fairy tale promise. All Kate had to do was run. She ran up the hill as fast as she could. Her heartbeats were heavy enough to hear. Kate hoped the sight of the hotel lights would persuade the driver behind to turn away. She looked forward to hearing the car drive past.

The car turned to follow Kate up the hill. The car increased its speed. The light around her feet spilled forward. She watched her legs turn pale.

I hope you realise that I can look after myself, she said.

Kate saw more clearly the outline of the hotel. The light from the hotel car park crept towards her and the tip of the beam from the car headlights. Kate told herself that once the light from the hotel reached the beam from the following car she would be safe. The final part of the hill was steep, and the few yards tested her legs. Kate tried really hard. The extra effort tired her but she reached the hotel car park quickly.

The lights and the hotel changed the world around her. She saw electricity, domestic comfort and, best of all, no disconnected outside. Kate was different, too. She was a proper adult again. She ran through the car park quicker than she expected. The hotel grew in front of her eyes, and she was able to see right through the windows and recognise comfortable secure people.

Kate turned her head around and looked. The car followed her into the car park. The headlight beam dipped into something sensible. The hotel entrance was only a few yards away when Kate stopped running. Walking, she was aware of being hot and breathless. Kate turned around and walked the last few yards to the hotel backwards. The panic alarm went back in her pocket. Her body remained warm and it was able to resist the winter cold. Listening to herself breathe, helped her relax. The car that had followed her found a parking space between others. The driver switched off the bright headlights. The glare from the lights in the car park made it impossible to see his face inside the car. She sat down on one of the steps at the entrance and waited. Kate suspected that if she danced around he would switch on his headlights again. Inside the hotel a loud person laughed more than the others did. The two lion statues either side of the hotel entrance stared beyond the car park and into the darkness.

I can't sit here all night, said Kate.

She stood up and leaned on one of the lions.

The driver stayed inside the car.

Kate took out her panic alarm and pressed the red button.

The noise may or may not have killed the conversation inside the hotel. The noise from the panic alarm was too loud for Kate to know. She left her finger pressed on the button. The car door opened, and the driver walked towards Kate. A hotel porter joined her in the doorway. Kate told him everything was all right and, as soon as she switched off the alarm, the porter disappeared back inside.

13

NATHAN SITTING ON A HOTEL STEP

I am sitting in the dark on a hotel step. Kate is sitting next to me. The car park is almost full. Either side of Kate and me are the two statues of lions that always wait in front of this hotel.

'You have to be clever, don't you, Nathan?' she says.

I have more stubble than normal. I brush back my dark hair with my hands. At the doorstep the night is half dark, and I hope that the strange light of the car park will ensure that I look handsome. I stretch my legs like someone ready for sleep. I am trying to be friendly. I want to be relaxed. Instead, I act tired.

'Nathan,' says Kate, 'how was I to know it was you?'

'Aren't you cold?'

'I'm too sweaty.'

'Ooh, right.'

'Don't push your luck, Nathan.'

'You weren't supposed to see me.'

'Your headlights were around my feet.'

'I thought I'd keep an eye out.'

I look over my shoulder at the hotel entrance behind.

'I'm not supposed to see you anymore,' says Kate. 'What should happen is that I only see you when we arranged, during the investigation.'

'I'm confused as to how long you are here.'

'Two more days, I'm seeing some friends.'

'Am I in trouble?'

'You'll find out. You knew I saw you. You were having a bit of fun.'

'Are you sure you're not too cold?'

'I'll have a warm shower in a minute.'

'Ooh, right.'

'Nathan, stop it. We can't act like we're kids.'

I watch Kate trace different lines on the carved mane of the nearest lion.

'We're not,' she says.

'What?' I say.

'We're not anything, Nathan. My investigation will be thorough and professional although brief. The problem with you, Nathan, is that your written reports can make any rubbish sound good.'

'I didn't intend to spoil your run.'

'Sooner or later, you must all go crazy down here. I would never settle for this. You shouldn't have, Nathan. You were the country boy that should have left.'

I watch Kate run her finger over the head of the lion on her side of the step. The car park lights make it clear that the lions have been painted black.

'I was daft running in the dark,' says Kate.

'There are better places to run,' I say. 'You can run along the river behind Buckland House. Start at the lodge and go as far as the ruins. In the dark, it looks like a collapsed abbey. It's quite picturesque.'

'It sounds creepy.'

'You'd be made welcome. The guardian angels sit by the riverbanks at night. Their hands trail in the water.'

'You're making this up, Nathan.'

'You're still healthy and in shape, Kate. I was in third gear at one point.'

'You look very smart, Nathan.'

I am very smart. I am wearing a red jacket, grey shirt and black trousers.

'I am seeing my girlfriend later,' I say.

'Aren't you a bit old for stubble?'

I stroke my face again.

'I hoped it would hide the bruise,' I say. 'I hope I don't get posted to London because of your thorough investigation. My girlfriend likes to enjoy herself. Spend what's left of my fortune.'

'If she's special, Nathan, it's only right.'

'I'm happy enough if she puts up with me.'

'We are talking about the ex-prostitute, right?'

Kate stops stroking the lion.

'Carl's story was horrible,' she says. 'I'm disappointed in you.'

'I didn't know you had hopes.'

'I didn't. You can still be disappointed.'

'If you stay outside, you may catch cold.'

'You should have left Adbury, Nathan. You should have had a career.'

'I'm doing all right for a damaged sociopath.'

'You were a decent copper, Nathan.'

'I was only ever clever. You are cold. Look at your legs.'

'You think I crept to get on.'

'If anybody ever did it with just intelligence and industry, I suspect it would be you, Kate.'

I pull my legs back until my feet touch the bottom step.

'I'm sorry I upset you before,' I say. 'I didn't mean to.'

'Nathan,' says Kate, 'why did you ever join the police?'

I grin and wink. I use my hands to brush my hair again. The truth is I know that she finds this attractive. I also have no intention of answering the question.

'You had to have your bit of fun with me,' says Kate.

'Fun?' I say, 'I normally beat up suspects for fun. Is this Thursday because I usually do so on a Thursday?'

Kate laughs, and I make an effort with my smile.

'These lions have different expressions,' says Kate. 'Perhaps not.'

I look at the lions closely.

'I've never noticed,' I say. 'Imagine having to settle for one mood for the rest of your life. Having to make a choice. It'd be worse than picking a career.'

'I have a feeling that's a dig,' says Kate.

'I'll see if I can find a route for you to run so you can keep out of the dark. Nantwich is worth a visit while you're down here.'

I look up at Kate.

'I'm sorry about Chris,' I say

'We didn't last that long, Nathan. He was the rebound from you. I knew that.'

Kate looks into the distance. She rubs her legs to keep them warm.

'It's not worth hanging around this step,' she says.

'It must be the effect of these bright lights,' I say. 'I don't like wasting them, if it's all right for the lions, eh? I wonder what mood they did pick.'

'You're crazy,' she says.

Kate does not say goodbye. I watch her turn and leave and walk away without turning back. There are now just two very unassertive lions and me. Because I like their uncritical nature, I remain with them on the wide concrete steps. I am reluctant to either go home or visit Esther who I know will tell me all about her interview with Kate and who will ask me all about mine. I think about Kate inside the hotel, walking to her room and taking a shower. Wherever Kate is, she cannot see me. I put my head in my hands.

14

NATHAN AND ESTHER IN BED AGAIN

I am in bed with Esther. I was right. There was an argument. Now, neither of us is sleeping. Esther may have her eyes closed. I do not know because the room is dark and because, of course, my own eyes are closed. She is, though, still talking. This has gone on a while. She is in single driver conversation cruise control. It happens after an argument.

'I reckon it's because she is glamorous and sophisticated,' says Esther. 'I bet you were head over heels.'

I keep my eyes closed and I stay where it is safer.

'I have the better figure,' says Esther.

You have the perfect figure, I think. She is a person, and you are a physical altar.

'She is very elegant. She has lots of poise.'

I am not tempted, Esther, I think. I will say nothing.

'She has something.'

The something in Kate was what I could talk to. I do not say this. I keep my eyes closed.

'She didn't ask about us. She mentioned it. She called you my boyfriend but she did not ask.'

The newly anointed boyfriend keeps his eyes closed.

'She's very work focussed.'

So you have said, Esther, a dozen times. I do not say this. I keep my eyes closed.

'She asked me where I bought my outfit.'

Jesus Christ, please rescue me.

'I have the better figure but I would like to be tall like her. She runs every day. She doesn't use a gym'.'

I am not sure if I hear something outside. Esther acts as if she has heard nothing. Maybe it is because I am lying in the dark with my eyes closed and listening to drivel that I am now hearing noises.

'She thinks she's too old for a gym', says Esther. 'I told her she could easily do a light circuit around my place.'

How did I manage to miss all this that has been happening, I think. I must see if I can buy the DVD. I say nothing. I keep my eyes closed.

'She knew I used an alias. I told her I had had a difficult past and I needed a change. I said that was why I had called the gym' New Beginnings.'

It occurs to me that this is what life is like without arguments; endless self-absorption and memory. Or maybe it is what follows life. I need to open my eyes but, if I do, we will only argue.

'I reckon she's a worrier,' says Esther.

I am convinced I hear another noise.

'No, keep your eyes closed, Nathan,' says Esther. 'I told her I worry, especially about Alex McGrath. 'I spend all day worrying about other people's bodies and all night worrying about going bankrupt,' I said.'

Esther laughs, as if she has said something witty. Well, by her standards, possibly she has. Maybe she should be given encouragement.

'Very clever,' I say.

Because I am lying, I keep my eyes closed.

'I reckon I'm all right with worry,' says Esther. 'Worry is better than depression. I'd rather have worry than arguments. I'm talking to you now, Nathan, not her.'

Talk to whom you want, I think. I'm keeping my eyes closed.

'She wore a nice charcoal grey suit. See, she can do that because she is tall.'

Death, I think, where are you?

'I was tempted to tell her I was seeing a psychiatrist,' says Esther. 'I reckon she knows you are.'

The nutcase keeps his eyes closed.

'She wore nice earrings. The tall don't get cellulite as quickly, you know.'

I know. The conversation is unbelievable.

I finally speak. 'Esther, I would like to go to sleep. I am not a glutton for the stuff but perhaps a few hours before work tomorrow.'

Esther switches on the light at the same moment as I open my eyes. My eyes burn a little.

'Not another argument, please,' I say.

'Did you hear something?' says Esther.

I say nothing. I am not being clever, I am obeying an implied instruction to listen. I hear a car door slam somewhere.

The loud bang is a surprise. The darkness behind the curtain becomes light, and outside stays bright. The room is filled with imitation daylight. Outside changes colour from white to orange and back again. A sudden roar that sounds like a bonfire follows the changes in colour. The noises that appear next are not as loud but they hint at explosions and breakage. I am anxious, really anxious.

'You stay there,' says Esther. 'You stay in bed where you can do no harm.'

15

NATHAN IN THE DOORWAY OF THE HOME OF ESTHER WELLES

I am standing where Esther had stood when I had called after she had returned from Spain. Esther appears at my side with a new looking fire extinguisher that she has found in the garage. On the drive a BMW something burns, and occasionally fittings in the car explode. The flames are high but point straight to the sky.

'No,' I say.

Esther moves to walk past me but I put my body between her and the open door. I take away the fire extinguisher. She looks at me as if it is me that has set the BMW on fire. I am tempted to smack her across the face with the fire extinguisher. Actually, I am not really tempted. True, this is a woman who has lodged an official complaint against me but the unexpected bonfire on the drive has teased out the pragmatist in me. Yet, as we stand staring at each other with hatred, I find it is more than easy to imagine the pleasure that smacking her over the head with something large and heavy would give me. I also think about how pleasurable it would be to continue thumping and to set about the neighbours. No reason why but it would be satisfying.

'You don't go anywhere near it,' I say. 'I've called the fire brigade. We wait for the experts.'

Esther grabs the fire extinguisher again.

'Let go,' I say, 'or I'll hit you over the head with it.'

Esther takes her hands off the fire extinguisher. I was unaware the thing existed. I tell myself I must have a proper look at what is inside her garage sometime. I am not sure if I have ever visited.

'There isn't a wind,' I say. 'The house will be safe. We've even got some drizzle but I will stay here and keep an eye. If it gets dangerous, I will use the extinguisher and then call you. Esther, go into the kitchen and make a cup of tea.'

'It's my car,' she says.

'The car is finished. If it threatens the house, I'll shout. Esther, I've got experience.'

Esther smiles.

'That's what I like about you,' she says. 'Whatever the circumstances, you never swear. I thought it made you different.'

'I'll watch the fire,' I say.

'If you weren't such a fucking bastard.'

I have not hit you with the fire extinguisher, I think. But I say nothing. Esther walks towards her kitchen to make herself a cup of tea. I have no hopes that she will think of making me one. The BMW whatever it is burns. Oddly, the car radio still plays. I listen to the DJ talk rubbish while he melts as well. His voice pleads for attention but that is not because he is on fire inside the exploded BMW. It is his nature, most probably. The front indicator lights on the BMW flash as they have done since we heard the loud bang and the roar of fire.

I look around the cul-de-sac. Most of the houses have at least one light switched on. No doubt, the neighbours will appear soon. The heat of the blaze makes my face warm, and the smoke leaves a strange taste in my throat. It irritates me but nowhere near as much as the idiot melting DJ with the half American voice. I close the front door to keep him quiet.

The telephone rings. I let it ring.

Esther walks into the hall from the kitchen. She is now wearing a dressing gown and she is holding a mug of tea. Neither has prevented tears. Outside, the flames look enormous and close. I am more anxious than I pretend. Esther sits on the bottom stair and stares at the ringing telephone. The BMW still burns, and I can just about hear faint noise from the melting DJ.

Esther answers the ringing phone.

'I'm all right,' she says. 'We're waiting for the fire brigade. Nathan is watching the fire. No, it's okay. I'll see you this afternoon. Don't worry, I have a plan.'

Esther puts down the phone.

'Who is that?' I say.

'No one,' she says.

'Who's calling you at two o'clock in the morning?'

'No one you know.'

'What plan?'

Esther ignores me and drinks tea. I open the front door and recognise the sound of a fire engine somewhere. I smile at Esther. I leave the door open. The neighbours must hear it as well because they now leave their houses. They walk slowly across the cul-de-sac. The neighbours look like people do when their sleep has been disturbed, tousled hair and ill-fitting nightclothes. They all walk at the same pace, as if they all want to arrive together at the front door. I think of Zombies but without the blood. I am not well disposed to these slow walkers. I do not assume it is that they are simply being curious. These are people who are checking if their prosperity and security is intact. I look at the fire extinguisher and confirm to myself that I want to smack a lot more than Esther. I think that is what I was doing in the scruffy hotel, somehow trying to smash through. To what, though, I do not know.

The fire engine arrives, and the neighbours wait in the road. Esther leaves the bottom stair and stands next to me. I notice that the voice of the burning DJ has disappeared. The early morning preacher has perished in the flames.

'Who was that on the phone?' I ask again.

'Fuck off,' says Esther.

Firemen leave the vehicle. They see the burning car and react. I watch them douse the flames with powerful hoses. They shout warnings to each other. The dying fire smells badly, so I shut the front door again. The zombies in the street watch and say or do nothing. Esther sips from her mug of tea. I am quite thirsty, myself, I think. Esther smudges away old tearstains so she is ready for the firemen.

The flames from the BMW disappear quickly. The car, drive and front walls of the house are drenched. The parts of the car not charred shine because they are damp and unblemished. Two of the neighbours cross the road that shapes the cul-de-sac. The others talk. A fireman stops the two neighbours and asks them to return to their homes or at least join the others.

'I don't deserve this,' says Esther.

Outside, the fireman nods and beckons me towards him.

'This bloke is a dope,' I say to Esther.

She takes the hint and returns to the kitchen. I step outside.

The fireman who has beckoned me outside is called Joe. I remember him from school. He was captain of the football team. He carries his yellow helmet as if it is a football and he is expecting a game.

'So that's the beauty you're knocking a slice off,' says Joe.

'That's the woman I dream about,' I say.

'We all do that, Nathan. You do something about it. The rest of us have wives that get in the way.'

I think of what I would rather not think about.

'Are you still playing football?' I say.

Joe shrugs. I have no idea what this means and I do not care.

'Do you want to have a look round the motor?' says Joe.

The BMW is drenched and finished but to keep Joe happy I walk around the ruin. Another fireman takes photographs on his mobile of the BMW whatever it was.

'Just as well there was no one inside,' says Joe.

'Only the DJ,' I say.

Joe thinks this an odd rather than mysterious remark. Joe has never been a friend. We always played in different football teams.

'Give my regards to the girlfriend,' he says.

His grin does not contain admiration.

The firemen board the vehicle and leave. The fire engine disappears. I look at my watch and wonder when the police will arrive. A neighbour leaves the rest and arrives at the BMW. He is wearing slippers with footballs sewn on the toes.

'I assume that you're the boyfriend,' says the neighbour with the footballs.

'No,' I say, 'I just visit to knock a slice off her.'

I turn and walk inside. As I close the door, I see the neighbour gesticulating to the others. I notice some shaking their heads. Let them think it through is my view.

Inside the living room, Esther is watching TV with the sound turned low.

'The neighbour thought I was your boyfriend,' I say.

'I hope you put him right,' says Esther.

'Oh, yes.'

'This isn't right, Nathan. I don't deserve this. I don't want to win battles. I just wanted somewhere to stay and maybe, for once, do well.'

'I'll phone the car insurance after the police have been.'

'Boyfriends should help someone to stay. It should be easier with a boyfriend. But you're no use, are you, to anybody who wants to stay?'

As someone prone to make the odd remark, I am reluctant to condemn this as inarticulate nonsense. I know what Esther means and have no inclination to disagree. Instead, I remember the neighbours edging forwards, anxious to know if everything can stay intact. I hear the police arrive.

16

NATHAN IN THE CAR PARK OF A LARGE HOTEL IN ADBURY

I am standing in the half full car park of the Barrel Park Hotel and Leisure Centre. The night is dark. I remember from school that the Spanish call these hours the *madrugada*, and the word suits the black sky well. I am holding a can of paint and a paintbrush. Both are large. I found them in the garage of Esther, which was more impressive than I expected although her large toolbox did make me feel inadequate. I saw the toolbox and remembered what she said about helping her to stay. Well, I cannot do that. This is more my style. I had hoped to find a can of yellow paint but there was none so I settled for green. I drop to my knees and put the can of paint down on the car park tarmac. I paint close to the entrance of the car park. Here, it will have more effect but I also want to be able to make an easy exit. I thought about this while I was driving to the hotel. What I would paint and even details about the size of the letters and whether I should use block capitals. I try to keep the writing neat. I do not use a torch because the letters I paint are large. Perfect for the *madrugada*, I think.

This is what I paint.

ALEX MCGRATH IS A CROOK THAT TERRORISES THE INNOCENT

It is a lot to paint in the darkness of the *madrugada* but I am not afraid. Alex McGrath can only hurt me again. But nobody comes. The people on the night shift stay inside the hotel. The empire of Alex McGrath sleeps. I am certain that I have not made any mistakes. I will never see these words. No doubt, they will be removed in daylight. But to ensure McGrath sees what I have written, I call the police as soon as I arrive at my home and I report the incident. The woman on the switchboard asks me for a description of the vandal. I tell her it was very dark and that it was not possible to see distinguishing features. The woman on the switchboard understands and is sympathetic. I tell her that even in the dark it appeared to me that the vandal was handsome.

17

NATHAN IS AGAIN IN THE DOORWAY OF THE HOME OF ESTHER WELLES

I lean against the doorframe from where I saw the BMW whatever it was burn to death.

I watch Carl arrive and park very neatly, next to the pavement, his police Mondeo. He walks past the dead BMW and stops at the front door.

'I'm not coming inside,' he says. 'I have to get ready for later and I want you there as well, Nathan.'

'Esther has gone for her courtesy car,' I say.

'I assume it was you that painted the car park of Alex McGrath.'

'Is there a description?'

'He was described as very handsome.'

'Sounds like me,' I say.

The day is winter mild but there is more wind than there was during the *madrugada* and it makes the strange white yellow hair of Carl lively and unruly.

'I hate all this, Nathan,' says Carl. 'I'm supposed to be introducing my detectives to the Chief Constable later. And that includes you. Maybe McGrath is right. Maybe the town would be better off without her. I really hope that you didn't paint his car park.'

'You're more worried about his car park than her house and car.'

'Esther does not keep Manchester gangsters at bay, and, if we had them, Nathan, we'd have Manchester coppers. Imagine their effect on the clearance figures. You're not right, Nathan. Even pretending to be crazy is crazy.'

'You should come inside.'

Carl smiles at a neighbour who is walking to her car.

'No, I've got to go and prepare. You must be on your best behaviour later. Promise me.'

'I won't say a word. I'll even breathe intermittently.'

'If I hear that you joke about being dead or say you're a ghost who's waiting to be a guardian angel, you're finished, Nathan.'

He stops to smile and wave at the neighbour who drives past.

'I'd settle for what you were like before,' says Carl, 'going on about books and being superior. All this Buckland House rubbish and ghost stuff wears people down, Nathan. Do you still carry the obituary?'

I think it best not to answer.

'I told you to get rid of it,' says Carl. 'Dr Long has told you to get rid of it.'

'You've been talking about me,' I say, 'you and her.'

Carl looks around the cul-de-sac. He lives in something similar so is probably not as impressed as me. He faces me with the same disdain as before.

'I am part of your therapy,' he says. 'We have to talk about you; Jesus, Nathan.'

'They reinvented me,' I say.

'Not again, someone give me strength.'

'I've nothing to look forward to.'

'I know, I understand.'

'I've been denied the perfect death.'

'I understand, Nathan. Dr Long has explained. It took time but I understood.'

Carl looks sideways, as if something interesting might be happening elsewhere.

'I was a hero in that obituary,' I say.

'I understand,' he says. This time he is louder than before.

'I know I can turn on people.'

'Don't we know. You've always had a temper. You got away with it because you had a sense of humour. Nobody laughs anymore.'

'Esther wants to work hard, to have a plan and a man she trusts. She said.'

'Spare me people with plans. Why don't they just get by and get what they can? Nathan, can't you persuade Esther that it's best she leaves?'

'It isn't best at all, Carl. Esther is getting a bad deal.'

'Kate is coming to the Conference.'

'I thought she'd finished the investigation.'

'She has. This is how Kate has fun. People like Kate never stop.'

'If it keeps her happy.'

'It doesn't. She was in the chemist asking for something to help her sleep. I talk to people, Nathan. I discover things.'

'That stuff should be confidential.'

'This is Adbury, Nathan. If she wants privacy, she should have stayed in Liverpool. Kate also suffers from continuous menstruation. I think she was in the chemist a while.'

'It is not right that you know this, Carl.'

'Why not? She's nosy and she's only coming because the Chief Constable is there.'

I am thinking about Kate. I hate the idea of her being successful but unhappy.

Carl has stopped thinking about Kate.

'Last night, I was even talking to my mother about the Conference,' says Carl. 'Not properly but we did talk.'

Carl puffs out his red cheeks.

'I have to go,' he says. 'Don't let me down, Nathan. Let's all try and get by.'

'You should come inside.'

'No, I've got to go.'

18

NATHAN AT THE RACES

I am standing against a wall facing a window behind which I can see the Chester racecourse. There are no horses just the green track and the white fence. I am tired and, like every other copper in the room, apart from Carl, I do not want to be here. On my wall are lined the detectives which is why I am there. On the opposite wall, standing with their backs to the racecourse are the uniforms. I hate all this. The seats in the large room are taken by the civilians – managers from outside the police and other worthies.

A large screen hangs from the ceiling at the front of the long room. Close to the blank screen there is a microphone and stand alongside a modern fabric covered podium.

Esther qualifies for an invite as a local businesswoman. She arrives after everyone else and while Carl is preparing himself behind the podium. She settles for a seat in the front row next to our psychiatrist and Kate who happens to be sitting next to Dr Long. This annoys me and makes me fearful. Somehow, Esther manages to be breathless and impeccable. All the men smile sympathetically. Carl lets the moment belong to Esther, waits until everyone has recovered before tapping the microphone.

The civilians laugh politely but the coppers stay silent. The uniform, podium and microphone make Carl look important. The creases in his uniform are fresh and sharp. Carl stands straight and poses, aspires to the effete integrity that always appeals to bosses. The people in the audience look as if they are dressed for a day in the office. I never trust Carl, even with the simplest tasks. I am nervous although none of this has consequence for me.

Carl presses the remote control hidden in his hand. On the screen behind him the image changes. Carl talks. I stare at Kate, Dr Long and Esther who are already smiling at one another as if they were all friends. Carl talks about customer service and the business plan and budgetary threats. I am not sure if he understands any of it but he has notes and he can read. Every so often he refers the civilians to their leaflets. Every time he mentions the Chief Constable he pauses before and afterwards. I really hate all this.

Somehow, it is over.

'We believe in a police force that provides a quality service. Thank you everyone.'

The civilians applaud. The uniformed policemen clap as well. Me and the other detectives limply put our hands together. Carl kisses his lips and blushes. He stands very still. Eventually, he takes a breath. The lecture has been typical Carl. He never impresses but always survives.

'Any questions?' he says.

Esther stands up before anyone else. Carl smiles, an expression that he has rehearsed, a willingness rather than confidence. Esther wears a quality two piece grey suit with a jacket cut short to reveal perfect hips. The suit I have never seen before. I am familiar with the hips.

Esther half turns around so the audience can see her.

'Esther Welles, New Beginnings,' she says. 'I own the fitness centre in the High Street. Carl, I see that all your detectives are here.' Esther turns her back on the audience, faces Carl again. 'Most of the criticism of the police from our own community is directed at particular detectives. Shouldn't they be on the stage taking questions.'

Kate turns her head to look at me. I shrug my shoulders.

Carl lets Esther sit down. He takes time to think it over and he also gives me a warning look. I shrug again. Who cares, I think. The familiar hips will soon be history.

'In the context of our overall service,' says Carl, 'the impact of our plain-clothes division on face-to-face service is somewhat marginal. Members of the public are much more likely to meet a uniformed policeman or policewoman. Most crime is investigated initially by our patrol officers. Perhaps because of that and, because we all have to start somewhere, I did not sufficiently stress the importance of the detectives in my speech but as you quite rightly point out the detectives are here and as you know,' Carl pauses, 'they are quite accessible.'

Some of the civilians laugh, and this makes Esther raise her head.

'Of course, in Adbury,' says Carl, 'we benefit from low crime and high detection. And no, we are not complacent.'

Esther thinks about saying more but decides against. Kate turns around to look at me again. This detective detects a hint of a smile. We can all be cynical but for Carl the training has worked. Esther does not bother him again. He answers a couple of other questions in a similar manner, admitting everything but nothing, mentioning the politically correct views and committing himself always to taking the views of the questioner on board. The audience stands up and heads for the foyer to drink coffee and eat Danish pastries. I hate all this.

Inside the foyer, Kate, Dr Long and Esther form a group to talk. I may be wrong but they look as if they are discussing the new suit that Esther is wearing. One thing is certain. She did not buy it to impress me.

Carl walks over to me and says hello. I am surprised because I expected him to be creeping somewhere.

'Well?' he says.

'What do I know?' I say. 'You're the performer, Carl. I'm just a work type.'

'I'm happy with a script. It's not important if you do it properly or not, as long as you do it. That's how CVs are built, Nathan.'

Listening to this is worse than thinking about the hips of Esther. The truth is that I would settle for her wearing the new suit as a defiant farewell gesture. Thinking that she is wearing it for the benefit of everyone else and not me leaves this detective feeling very alone.

Carl is still talking. 'The owner from the Little Picture House is here. He's giving out leaflets. He asked me to sign his petition. I said I couldn't, not while I am acting in an official capacity.'

I am not really listening. I am watching Esther, Kate and Dr Long talk and laugh. Dr Long eats an éclair. Kate and Esther sip coffee. They all look in my direction and wave at me. I nod hello and the expressions on their three faces harden. I know that if Carl disappears I will be left standing here alone until all this nonsense finishes.

Carl is still talking. After last night, I am grateful for his company.

'Esther,' he says, 'has registered as a family friendly employer.'

I say nothing.

I am tempted to drink some coffee.

'Esther told me,' says Carl. 'I presume you knew.'

'I'm just a bloke who used to knock a slice off her,' I say.

'Nathan, that's the best way. The sooner she's gone the better.'

Kate, Esther and Dr Long are still staring at me. I remember the dog sitting in the rain at Barrel Park Hotel and Leisure Centre. The dog and these three people have the same look on their faces.

'Esther hasn't gone yet,' I say.

'She will,' says Carl. 'McGrath will win. We don't want Esther to win. High detection and low crime.'

'You're just thinking about your career.'

'I'm thinking about us getting by. I want a quiet life. I worry about my mother and I worry about you.'

'Carl, you sound as if you're preparing us both for death. Maybe that's why you've done well in Adbury. Like me, you enjoy mingling with the dead.'

'The bloke who owns the cinema calls his dog Leone.'

'Sergio would be too Italian,' I say. 'Carl, you should circulate.'

'Do I have to? I've had a terrible night with my mother and everything. You should talk to Kate and your psychiatrist.'

'They're paid to talk to me. They don't need courtesies.'

'Kate is still here, Nathan.'

'She's seeing her friends.'

'She looks like a woman waiting for a sniff.'

I look at the three women again. They are still together and talking. They all look at me and they smile but in a way that says I am not needed. The sight of so many people standing around, sipping drinks and making conversation makes me think of the night when the bomb dropped on Buckland House. Without Carl nagging, I would have been able to retreat and become a ghost. Now, the three women stare at me but it would be easy for me to disappear without consequence. If I was not a detective, I could even be a guardian angel. I imagine existence without work and without me being obliged to knock a slice off anyone. The three women continue talking. The expressions on their faces, though, have changed. Esther is now hostile, Dr Long has regret and Kate is occupied with mystery.

'Carl,' I say, 'you should be talking to the worthies, not me.'

'I'm more worried about you,' says Carl.

'I understand.'

The three women are still staring at me. As before, Kate is the least hostile but none are friendly.

The coffee break finishes. Carl returns to the stage, and we all head to where we were. The rest of the short afternoon is the usual syndicate exercises. The worthies are asked about their expectations from a professional police force. I hate all this. I wonder if I should have said something about Kate. I assume she will be leaving tomorrow. I think about Buckland House and the night the bomb dropped. I imagine well-groomed aristocrats on festive heat, flirting, active and confident but also anxious, going to their deaths and thinking about what they have left unsaid.

As soon as Carl thanks everyone in his farewell speech, Esther stands up before the rest and heads for the exit. She smiles as if her rudeness is an alternative grace. I wait until she disappears from the hall and follow. While Carl was speaking, I saw Esther send a text so I am suspicious. I see her outside. She is standing next to her car. A car park attendant looks at Esther as if he has just discovered a new fantasy figure. If I were a proper guardian angel, I would float over towards him and pull him away so he can stare at something safe. Instead, like the car park attendant, I stand and gaze at Esther. In the suit, she looks fabulous. I will definitely miss those hips. Another woman drives a Ford Focus into the car park. She parks next to Esther and her courtesy car. The woman leaves her car. She is a distance away but I recognise her because the time I saw her before she was also a distance away. It is the woman that I saw from the window in the gymnasium, the woman whose appearance startled Esther and who, I thought, made McGrath gloat. Esther and the woman talk. I step back into the foyer of the racecourse entrance. Esther is giving the woman instructions. I am convinced of this, which is odd because I do not know what to think anymore.

19

NATHAN DRIVING
HIS FORD FIESTA

I am in my car, driving and listening to the news headlines on Radio 4. It is late afternoon but already dark. I am driving home but I have taken the longest route possible because I hate arriving home bewildered, and what I saw in the car park has confused me. My route amounts to a scenic tour of rural Cheshire. Indeed, if I were a responsible and caring person, I would recommend it to others. But, as should be clear by now, responsibility is not ingrained in my nature. I do not think of how I might benefit others but brood on what Esther was doing.

The news on the Radio does not help. The BBC announcer is excited about a scientific discovery. I switch off the radio and swallow some of the darkness that is outside. The trees look like they do late at night. They lean forward, as if ready to pounce. The premature darkness and the silence irritate my nerves. I take a bend too late but recover by braking where I should not. Without the radio to listen to, I pick up speed. There are two explanations for the scene in the car park. McGrath brought the woman to Adbury but somehow Esther has managed to do a deal with her. The alternative is that McGrath was telling the truth when he said the woman was a stranger and that Esther was acting daft in her gym'. This option, though, confuses me. If that is the case, none of it makes sense – the woman, the yellow paint and the exploding car.

In the dark, I mutter to myself, reconsider the arguments for and against each option. Either way, I am angry with Esther and I was not exactly feeling friendly before. I have a grievance, which, in the darkness, feels intense. I regret not going home immediately. I feel tired and think an alcoholic drink, a comfortable chair and perhaps a look again at some of the Buckland House files are preferable to thinking about Esther. But, of course, my damned brain persists. I make myself angry thinking about her treachery and her accusing me of allowing her to be a victim. Okay, I can be a little cold and self-obsessed but I have never told her lies. Of course, one can never be certain.

A pair of headlights on the other side of the road makes me blink and feel tired. The other cars appear intermittently. The rest is the usual, dark road, strange trees, rolling tarmac and the persistent white line. I stop at a T-junction without traffic lights. The headlights of the Fiesta pick out the sign hiding in the hedge. Stoke to the right, and Nantwich to the left. Right for Shropshire, and left for Cheshire. I remember how Kate always used to moan about every sign pointing to Nantwich. I turn left. As I pull on the steering wheel, I think about the treachery of Esther and my own to Kate and my family. I hate myself.

I carry on driving, stay friends with the white line and think of the road as possible Novocaine. Rain arrives on the windscreen in three phases. Light, heavy and really heavy. I use all three speeds on the windscreen wipers. The few cars that pass, they all have flashing wipers. The rain in their headlight beams is bright and alive. I should have gone straight home. I let a row of cars pass by before turning on my headlights to full. The driver behind me does the same. I react quickly and pull the rear mirror down.

The driver behind presses his horn.

What's the likelihood you are on holiday? I say to myself.

The headlights behind me appear as a reflection in my windscreen, two white circles. The windscreen wipers flash back and forth.

Show some respect, I mumble to myself in the dark. For once, I quote the rules of my betters. Keep your distance, I say.

I listen to the rain hit the roof of the Fiesta. I note the sharp thumps against the metal and remember that Congleton had been flooded a month earlier. The town had been drenched with a month of rain in half an hour.

This weather makes as much sense as the latest scientific discovery that has the *BBC* excited, I think.

I put my foot down on the accelerator. I drive the Ford Fiesta around a couple of bends faster than I would have liked. At the side of the road, trees zoom in towards me. The tyres, though, make a smooth noise, and the white circles from the car behind stay in my windscreen. As soon as the road is straight, I turn around to look. The headlights behind are high above the road. The motor is some kind of four-wheel drive. The motor stays close. I turn my head away quickly and catch sight of another car on the other side of the road. The driver in the other car slows down to look at the four-wheel drive.

This must resemble a car rally, I think. This is harassment.

I speak to the two circles reflected on the windscreen; you're going to kill someone.

As soon as I speak to them, they look different, more alert. I deliberately cross the white line in the middle of the road. Behind me the four-wheel does the same. The two vehicles come back to the side of the road. The four-wheel is close enough for me to hear it. The powerful engine is smooth and confident. I imagine the driver being something similar.

I focus on the road ahead. I am determined not to lose my temper and I start shouting, which I can do easily when driving. I switch on extra air to help clear the windscreen of mist. The inside of the car becomes hot and stuffy. The white circles in the windscreen ignore the extra air and heat and they remain calm.

The four-wheel drive keeps close. The driver resists pressing his horn again. The rain stops being stupid and settles for something almost normal. The windscreen wipers now look and sound silly, and I return them to normal speed. I listen to the rain on the roof but only occasionally.

The extra air inside the Fiesta is warm enough to make me sweat. When I have to change down gear for a bend, the sweat between my fingers makes my hand stick to the plastic gear knob. The four-wheel drive edges even closer. In my mirror, the smaller white circles grow in size. There are white circles wherever I look. The bumper of the four-wheel almost touches the Fiesta. The white circles in the windscreen hardly move. I hope the driver behind is a little more agitated than the white circles.

I pass the familiar left turn to my home, which I can see in the distance. The estate is lit by a pattern of street lamps. I do not want to be followed there. I watch my house and the street lamps disappear from view. Heading back into darkness, I wish I could have been a better person.

I make an extra effort for the sake of the Fiesta. I keep the seventy miles per hour as smooth as I can. On the other side of the road, more cars pass by. I flash them all, fake useless SOS. In the dark and with the lunatic behind, nobody would ever see my number-plate. A couple of idiots flash back in return. The driver behind sounds his horn.

This is tedious or it would be if it were not so worrying, I think.

As soon as the last of the cars has rushed by, I drive one-handed. I use my free hand to drag my mobile phone out of my jacket. Inevitably, the phone catches in the lining, and I am struggling. I complain about something but manage not to curse the phone. If anything, I speak quietly.

The mobile phone says nothing.

I am still struggling. I hope and blink which is more than the mobile phone does. It falls out of my jacket and into my lap. I change gear quickly and pick up the mobile phone. I hold the phone against the top of the steering wheel. My hands are sticky and clumsy. I press the phone menu button with my thumb. The usual light appears. I drive around a bend one-handed. I hear the four-wheel drive stay close.

Before dialling 999, I put the mobile phone next to my ear to listen to the tone.

The phone rings without warning. Inside the car, it sounds louder than I expect. I meet another bend and have to change gear one-handed. My mobile phone repeats a verse of the William Tell overture. I breathe my way out of the bend. The four-wheel drive does the same. I imagine the driver not having to make an effort.

I forget William Tell and remember the Lone Ranger. Right now, either would come in handy.

The road ahead is straight for as far as I can see. The two sets of headlights make the road look almost urban, like a stretch of half-bright road on the edge of town. I think about William Tell and if he ever had a horse. An ordinary horse, nothing special like Silver.

I take a deep breath, press the receive button on the phone and press it against my ear.

'Nathan, listen to me,' says the voice on the phone.

'I'm not sure if I'm capable,' I say.

The next bend arrives quicker than I expect.

'It's difficult to talk,' I say.

I cope with the bend quite well. I hear the four-wheel drive breathe all over the Fiesta.

'I know you're driving,' says the voice on the phone.

'It's awkward,' I say.

'I know. You've just changed gear.'

I pass a couple of cars and rain dripping trees.

'Alex,' I say.

'On these roads and in these conditions you don't do more than fifty,' says Alex.

I take my foot off the accelerator. The speed of the Fiesta drops to fifty miles per hour. The white circles on the windscreen stay the same size. The rain on top of the car becomes louder.

'That's it,' says Alex. 'Do as I say and you'll be safe.'

'Alex, this strikes me as obsessive,' I say. 'I don't understand why you can't leave me alone.'

The white circles became pale and small. My eyes heal almost immediately. I adjust the rear mirror back to its normal position. The headlights may now be normal but the four-wheel drive still drives too close.

'You get one of these motors, Nathan,' says Alex McGrath. 'Do something with your money. I can see everything from up here.'

I peer into my rear mirror. Alex McGrath is no more than a vague shape in the dark but the shape is recognisable. The four-wheel drive slips back a few yards.

'Listen, it's better friendly,' says Alex McGrath. 'You coppers should do advance driving.'

'I thought I did quite well,' I say.

I wipe one of my hands on my trousers.

'You want to feel the suspension on these four-wheels,' says Alex McGrath. 'The power steering is first class.'

'If it makes you happy to think that,' I say.

'Don't get funny, Nathan.'

His voice pauses. I can hear Alex McGrath breathe.

'Nathan, dip your lights,' says Alex McGrath. 'There's a van coming.'

I do as I am told but I am late, and the driver on the other side of the road presses his horn.

Alex McGrath waits until the van passes by. He comforts himself with a chuckle.

'Nathan, what are we doing in Shropshire?' says Alex McGrath.

'We must have lost our way,' I say. 'It's comforting to know you're behind me, Alex.'

'Don't be clever, Nathan.'

I imagine Alex McGrath driving without blinking or smiling, the eyes pale and smaller than normal. I make a serious attempt to see Alex properly.

'What happens if I call for reinforcements?' I say.

'I'll drive on top of your motor for a laugh,' says Alex McGrath. 'Don't be pathetic, Nathan.'

I look around the inside of the tiny Fiesta. His threat would not take any effort at all. The road turns into a dual carriageway.

'Increase your speed, Nathan,' says Alex McGrath.

The two lanes merge into one. The rain is still heavy. Alex McGrath waits until the road is clear again.

'Nathan, put your headlights back on,' he says. 'I don't like it with your dips on. It's a bit creepy.'

I am weary from being irritated. I need a break from the noise of the rain, the four-wheel drive splashing along as if it owned the road, the two engines echoing each other as if they are friends.

'You're going to tell me it's lovely and pretty in the daylight,' I say.

'I wasn't going to say anything,' says Alex McGrath.

I take the next bend too fast. The mobile phone falls into my lap. More dual carriageway appears, and the two vehicles increase speed. I overtake cars, and Alex follows, manages to offend a BMW and a Mercedes. Alex almost runs out of dual carriageway, and, for a moment, I have the hope that the four-wheel might crash. I put the phone next to my ear again.

'Don't do that again,' says Alex McGrath.

The road is straight again and narrow.

'Listen, Nathan,' says Alex McGrath, 'only do what I say. If you don't, I'll run you off the road and do something nasty. Don't be daft enough to fancy your chances.'

'I'm struggling to understand how in these circumstances I somehow give offence,' I say.

'Slow right down, then.'

The two vehicles drive along politely for a couple of miles. I keep the phone next to my ear.

'Turn right into this road,' says Alex McGrath.

'It's a forest drive,' I say.

'I can read, Nathan, full headlights, now.'

'It'll be pitch black.'

You have to have your way, Alex, I think.

The forest drive is single lane only. The trees hang over the drive, touch one another and obliterate most of the sky. The headlight beam makes the road below the trees look pale and ghostlike.

'Enjoy the peace and quiet, Nathan,' says Alex McGrath. 'Here, go into the next clearing.'

I find something on the right within the next few yards. The clearing has a very recognisable car park. The Forestry Commission sign next to the rubbish bin says, 'Polk Forest'. The two cars roll along gravel and stop side by side. I listen to the over two-litre engine being switched off and I do the same for the probably embarrassed Fiesta. The two vehicles are close together and quiet. Headlights are extinguished, and the forest disappears into darkness. The wind and the rain make a gentle persistent noise. I switch on the small light inside the car.

'Don't do that, Nathan,' says Alex McGrath,

I move to take the phone away from my ear.

'Don't do that, Nathan,' says Alex McGrath 'Just keep still. It's so quiet.'

I sit in darkness and listen to the wind and rain and the invisible trees pretending to be alive. It is quiet but not so quiet. Right now, a convenient apocalyptic holocaust would not go amiss.

'This is pretty in the daytime,' says Alex McGrath.

Who cares, I think.

'It's a picnic spot,' says Alex McGrath.

My eyes become used to the dark, and I am able to make out slight gaps between the trees.

'Understand, Nathan,' says Alex McGrath, 'I'm very effective at terrifying people. What about you?'

'I doubt if I am as effective as you,' I say.

I want to take the phone away from my ear.

'I'm not here so you can take the piss, Nathan,' says Alex McGrath. 'You're the type who likes his own company. Just a good book.'

'Not always.'

'I forgot. Life and soul of the party, are we?'

'I can sometimes be cheerful.'

'Cracking jokes all the time. That's Nathan.'

I do not crack jokes. I could not remember a joke to save my life.

'I thought we'd hear birds singing,' I say.

'It's either a crowd or nothing,' says Alex McGrath. 'The birds sometimes herd at night.'

Alex McGrath is quiet, whether he is trying to hear birds sing, I do not know.

'Nathan, say something,' says Alex McGrath.

'Would you accept common sense as sufficient argument against the idea of infinity?' I say.

'You have to be clever, Nathan. You thought you were being clever when you painted my fucking car park.'

'I heard about that.'

'I'll make you suffer, really suffer. I'll nail your feet to the floor.'

I listen while I look around the darkness. It is difficult to believe it goes on forever.

'I always know where you'll be,' says Alex McGrath. 'I found you soon enough this time.'

'Alex, I'd best get going,' I say.

'I've lived in Adbury all my life, Nathan. I want the best for it.'

I turn my mouth away from the mobile so Alex McGrath cannot hear what I say.

'Nathan, you will understand me,' says Alex McGrath. 'You will co-operate. Nathan, take off the central locking. Close your eyes.'

'What are you going to do, Alex?' I say.

'What I have to.'

I touch different parts of my face. I have this strange desire to remember it before more damage is inflicted. I am afraid, and that is why I close my eyes.

'Just what is it about thumping me that reassures you so much, Alex?' I say.

'I don't know,' says Alex. 'There must be something.'

I hear a door open.

'Alex, I can't see the sense in this,' I say.

'Stay still, Nathan,' says Alex McGrath. 'Keep your eyes closed. Put the phone down now. This is in case you don't think I'd nail your feet to the floor.'

What is all this rubbish about nailing feet to the floor, I think. I assume it is on his mind because he is still waiting for his dance floor. I keep my eyes closed. I hear a door shut. I lean my head back against the headrest. I switch off my mobile and use the remote control on my key ring to cancel the central locking. In the dark the locks opening sound like dogs barking. I hear footsteps disturb gravel. Footsteps make me think of feet being nailed to the floor. I keep my eyes closed.

The door to the Fiesta opens. The air from outside is colder than I expect, and the rain is quieter. I recall reading that it is impossible to smell the rain. The smell rain creates is no more than earth being disturbed. I listen to Alex sit down next to me. I am aware of his bulk. His anger surrounds me or so it seems. The first bang comes from somewhere around the back of my head. I picture the headrest exploding. I hear more bangs. I keep my eyes closed and imagine trees outside being blown out of the ground by dynamite.

The bangs stop, and my head aches. I am surprised to be still awake. The bangs have happened very quickly. I am impressed despite being in pain.

'I'm quick, aren't I?' says Alex McGrath.

I remember Alex McGrath talking about butting telegraph poles. If he is ever interested in trees, there are plenty here, and all are a preferable alternative to me.

'I am when I'm angry,' says Alex McGrath. 'Just remember.'

When he is not thumping people, Alex McGrath is really boring. Obviously, boredom is preferable, I tell myself.

This pain is endurable, I think. Not as awful as the queasiness I had to endure on past occasions when, because of Alex and Carl, I was obliged to look the other way.

Alex leans across me, presses the button in the door that

operates the electric window. This time I feel friendly rain. I turn my head towards the rain and I realise how much my face aches. I taste blood on my tongue, suspect one of the bangs has been a thump in the mouth. I keep my eyes closed. My right eye throbs enough to warm the eyelid. I dismiss the idea of retaliating because I fear the animal inside Alex and because I know brutality other than my own would prevail. No, I will pick my moment and I will have weapons.

Alex touches one of my bruises, one of my eyelids flickers and twitches.

'You'll live,' says Alex McGrath. 'Or you will, providing you don't paint any more fucking car parks.'

I lean my head back against the headrest. I keep my eyes closed.

'Cry if you want to,' says Alex McGrath.

'I can't see the point,' I say.

'I won't think any the worse of you.'

I let my eyelids burn.

'Use your mobile to get help,' says Alex McGrath.

'I'll drive home,' I say. 'I'm assuming I'm not dead.'

'Stop mumbling, Nathan.'

'My lips are swollen.'

Alex McGrath wipes blood away from my face with his hand. He uses paper, which I assume is newspaper.

'Realise you're like the rest of us,' says Alex McGrath. 'You have to behave. I'm telling you.'

'You realise you have assaulted a policeman?' I say.

'Not a real policeman, not anymore, Nathan.'

Time passes. Alex is reluctant to leave. I hope that he is not thinking about feet and nails.

'Have you any tissues to stop the bleeding?' says Alex McGrath.

I presume he has been staring at my wounds.

'I can't bleed forever,' I say.

'If you behave, this will be as rough as it gets,' says Alex McGrath. 'You wait till I go. You keep your eyes closed and mouth shut, and I won't nail your feet to the floor.'

He was thinking about it, I think.

I keep my hand over my eyes. I listen to the different sounds of outside. Rain drifts through the window and on to my face. The car door opens and closes. Footsteps make their way across the gravel. The forest is quiet and still but I can hear it breathe. It no longer pretends. I hear Alex climb into his four-wheel drive. I stop trying to listen. I think about being healed and cared for. I hear the tyres of the four-wheel move around in the gravel.

I take my head off the headrest and open my eyes. My neck is stiff and sore. I watch the four-wheel drive leave the clearing and join the forest road. The writing on the spare wheel cover says 'BARREL PARK LUXURY HOTEL ADBURY.' The spare wheel quotes the number of available rooms. The rear red lights dwindle away to nothing. Alex thumps his horn a couple of times before he disappears. Who decides these animals should prevail and have influence? It is a rhetorical question and the type you ask when you sit alone in the middle of nowhere and bleed.

It occurs to me that Alex might be losing control and that he has not enough imagination to hit anyone but me, which is definitely worrying. The dark is disturbing but peaceful. I imagine myself fading away to nothing like the red rear lights on the four-wheel drive. The good news is I have feet, and they are a weight on the floor. I will not fade away to nothing.

Twice, I think. This has happened twice. I think again of my solid feet being nailed to the floor. Twice, I mumble through swollen lips. Twice is unacceptable.

20

NATHAN IS STANDING IN A DOORWAY YET AGAIN

I am standing opposite the door of the hotel room of Kate. I have appeared a lot in doorways recently. Kate opens the door. She is wearing an ankle length dressing gown and has a towel wrapped around her head. She looks elegant. I am weary and in pain.

'You're running out of face,' says Kate.

I say nothing. Why should I? I have eloquent bruises.

'You have responsibilities to the neighbourhood, Nathan,' says Kate. 'Maybe you should stay indoors.'

'I'm not that good talking in doorways,' I say.

Although, to be fair, I have had practice. Kate does not take the hint. She leans against the doorframe. She uses a hand to flatten the towel on her head. I think that under the towel and the dressing gown she will be really clean.

'You're not going to go away,' says Kate, 'are you?'

The hallway I stand in is long and wide with thick carpet wall to wall. I hear lift doors open and close behind me.

'I wanted to see you before you left,' I say.

'You saw me,' says Kate. 'You harassed me when I went out for my run.'

'I want to wish you well

'You want me to treat those bruises.'

'If I could just rest.'

I think how pleasant it would be just to sit in a chair and watch her dress for the evening, watch her blow dry her hair. Kate turns away, and I follow her inside.

'I'll dry your hair,' I say.

My eyes plead.

'You wouldn't do it properly,' says Kate. 'Lie on the bed and say nothing.'

I do as Kate says. She adjusts massive pillows so I am comfortable. I lie there and watch Kate remove the towel from her head. Even though her hair is short, I expect it to tumble forth as perhaps the hair of Esther would. Her hair is wet and it looks even shorter than when I saw her outside her hotel. I am happy, though, to lie and watch Kate dry her hair. There is a substance to her that I have missed. I imagine her thinking calmly about her plans. She looks like someone who always has something serious in her head. The hotel room has a small table. Her laptop has the lid open. Kate sees that I have noticed.

'I wasn't working,' she says. 'I shouldn't tell you but I was curious about Buckland House. I was told about your obsession. I was curious.'

Kate sits sideways on a chair in front of a dressing table with a huge mirror. Her dressing gown parts so I can see her calves and the top of her thighs. Please let me watch you dress, I think. I do not ever want to leave, so I talk. Kate turns away and faces the dressing table mirror.

'I keep a photograph of Armstrong Taylor-Fielder,' I say. 'I cut a jagged edge through the middle, so it ran through his neck.'

Kate switches off the hair dryer and, in the mirror, she stares back at me. She shakes her head, and her short hair moves.

'It was how he died,' I say. 'A sheet of glass from the great window in the main hall sliced right through his neck.'

Kate switches the hair dryer on again.

'Nathan,' she says, 'just what are you doing in the police?'

'I suppose you have to spend your holidays somewhere,' I say.

'Then you should have taken it seriously.'

'After that gang took me away, working in the police was never the same again. It always felt like I was making a comeback and I was being compared with what I had been.'

Kate looks at herself in the mirror as she dries her hair.

'You need to move on,' she says.

I am always reluctant to talk about responsibility.

Instead, I say, 'The Taylor-Fielders were a pretty bunch. They had everything really. But they all had to die. He had to have his head cut off by a sheet of stained glass window.'

My feet point towards the bottom of the bed and my toes are close to the underwear that she will wear that evening. I want to know whom she will be seeing but I do not ask.

Kate looks towards her open laptop and she puts down her hair dryer.

'The Taylor-Fielder family wasn't anything special,' she says, 'so I heard, just rich.'

'Who knows?' I say. 'It takes a second to remember a life but infinity to understand it. If you're curious, all you have to do is pick a particular life and read. That's what our guardian angels do. Spend an eternity watching over us, trying to understand and help.'

Kate switches off the hair dryer and leaves it on the dressing table.

'But we die, Nathan,' she says.

'It's not the same for our guardian angel,' I say. 'For him, our moment is like a dream that lasts forever.'

'No wonder you get beaten up.'

'I have all kinds of books on Buckland House. I have books about the bombs that were discovered afterwards, others I have are about the family. I have photographs and files.'

Kate lets her bare feet swing in the air.

'I took the kids there,' I say. 'I picked up a leaflet and then felt obliged to read a book. I became an expert without intending. Now, I'm obliged to retain my expertise.'

'Obligations?' says Kate. 'You dumped me, Nathan.'

She stares into the dressing table mirror.

'I missed you,' I say. 'I needed something. When you meet other people interested in Buckland House, you feel human and harmless.'

'Harmless Nathan Wrench, as if.'

'Before the Taylor-Fielders were destroyed, everybody thought that they were the idle rich feeding off everyone. Once they were dead, they were impossible to explain. They were missed.'

I watch Kate sort her make-up. She wears little make-up, and what she wore I never noticed.

'When you went, my marriage collapsed,' I say, 'as if you had been the air in the paper bag.'

'That's awful, Nathan,' says Kate. 'You were using us both.'

My smile in the mirror looks as if it has been stolen from a vampire movie.

'Mrs Taylor-Fielder was rumoured to never have looked in a mirror,' I say. 'The night of the bombing, one of her daughter's new boyfriends bought her a mirror as a present and had insisted. The mother had not seen herself in the mirror until then. She wanted no vanity, nothing to haunt her. All this was before the stained glass sliced Armstrong Taylor-Fielder in two.'

Kate says nothing, looks in the mirror.

'I sometimes think I'm only a ghost myself,' I say. 'It's better than being a werewolf. With a ghost there's no hair or anything.'

'I should have offered you a cup of tea.'

'I'm not thirsty,' I say.

'That doesn't matter,' says Kate. 'It's a courtesy.'

'I'm not at my best, Kate. I'm injured.'

'It's not right you being so interested in ghosts. How long do Taylor-Fielder spirits last?'

'I assumed forever.' I hesitate and stammer. 'The home was hit by more than one bomb. The Germans confused their targets, thought they were bombing something else. I've found an Internet site that collects jokes about the disaster. It's somebody local but I can't work out who it is.'

'Maybe I should make some tea. You should find someone daft enough to look after you. '

'Kate, I'm sorry if I frightened you the other night.'

'I'd be happier if you looked after yourself.'

'I'm on your side, Kate.'

I pause and look at Kate who is now sitting with her back to me. Her back is long and straight. I remember the touch of her skin, which was always cooler than the skin of others.

'Can I watch you dress, Kate?' I say.

'You want to watch a half naked forty year old,' says Kate. 'How twisted is that?'

'Please.'

'Fuck off, Nathan. I am well used to selfish wrecks, and, physically damaged or not, you are as self-centred as ever.'

'We're not friends anymore?'

'You don't have any friends, Nathan.'

'We were friends once.'

'No, Nathan, never, I only ever admired you and I got that wrong.'

'We are not all driven like you, Kate.'

'Don't sneer at me.'

'Kate, there isn't a moment that your authenticity does not make me feel inadequate.'

'Nathan, you are now a policeman that people can thump with impunity. You've no idea how contemptible that is. And you want to watch me dress?'

'I want to do more than that, Kate.'

Kate says nothing. I continue to stare at her back.

'I have to go out soon,' she says.

'Me, too,' I say. 'I have my farewell meeting with Esther.'

'No wonder you are feeling sorry for yourself.'

I say nothing. I stare at the back that does not move and I imagine her cool skin. I wait for Kate to ask me to leave. Minutes pass before Kate surprises me. She not only turns around, her eyes are moist.

'It would never have worked, Nathan,' says Kate. 'You're not the type to follow a woman's career around the country. The world has to revolve around you.'

Seeing Kate without the dressing gown is becoming an obsession. I think about possible compromises, minimum bare flesh that could be acceptable.

'Aren't you bored down here?' I say. 'These are not nice people, Kate.'

'They're just slow thinking,' says Kate.

'Carl is not fit to be a Superintendent, and I've gone bandit.'

'Carl is tied to the house and his mother.'

'He wastes his life flicking around satellite channels all night. She can't watch a full programme, so he flicks around to stop her being bored.'

'Daft as it sounds, I think that's devotion.'

'The police is not a proper job, Kate.'

'It beats waiting for the tea trolley. I met the Chief Constable in Chester. He's really smooth.'

'You wonder how some people get so smooth.'

'He'll have special polish. He's a bit slimy. I hope I'm not like that.'

Kate stands up and walks to the wardrobe. She takes out a dress.

'You'll have to go,' she says.

I look at the dress and I imagine the two of us together. I am desperate to see and touch something other than what I can.

'Nathan, you once made a difference,' says Kate.

She moves the dress and her underwear to the chair in front of the dressing table. She takes one of my pillows, puts it behind her head and lies down beside me. She touches the bruises on my face with the tips of her fingers. Her fingers, of course, do not have the cool skin I remember. That is elsewhere, inside the dressing gown. We look at our reflection in the mirror.

'I worry about the last promotion,' says Kate. 'The people at my level are slimy. All my career I've had to bounce between the slime and the slobs.'

'I'm a slob?' I say.

'You were never slimy.'

'Slimy feet should squelch.'

The words slimy and squelch make me think of sex.

'Esther is very pretty,' says Kate.

'Was in my case,' I say.

'She makes me feel like an old hag. She's all smiles.'

'Not a slob, then?'

'In Adbury, you can't tell the slobs from the slime. When I applied for the police, I asked my father what he wanted me to do. 'See it through,' he said.'

'Down here, we like every week to be like the last one.'

'You wonder what they look forward to.'

'The company of their friends, we all need somebody to help us relax. I was hoping you could keep me out of mischief, Kate.'

She leaves the bed and takes her clothes from the chair by the dressing table. She puts them down at the foot of the bed. I notice some cleavage appear above the lapels of her dressing gown. It is not my ambition but it will have to suffice.

'No,' says Kate without looking at me. 'Nathan, you're beyond help.'

21

NATHAN INSIDE THE BIG GREEN ONION

I am sitting in the Green Onion, the largest and most popular pub in Adbury. Esther and me share a small drink packed table.

'Nobody is listening to this music,' I say.

'So you've said,' says Esther.

'They're nodding their heads, though.'

'So you've said.'

'Nodding heads do not have to mean anything.'

'So you've said.'

'The other pubs are empty.'

'So you keep saying.'

'I'm not going to be frightened by Alex McGrath.'

'Your face is embarrassing. If I'd known, I wouldn't have turned up. I've seen zombies with less damage.'

'They really exist?' I say.

'I mean films,' says Esther.

If there were observers, it would be apparent to them that our evening is not going well. I am drinking as quickly as I can and I am already drunk. The Green Onion has a history. It is seventeenth century, and horses and coaches once rested there on their journey from the North to London. Despite the cold winter wind, the two entrance doors are open. The pub has dark brown walls and a high roof. Metal posts are dotted around the empty wooden floor and they support the high roof. The few tables that do exist are pushed against the walls and some are loaded with upturned chairs. Posters, posted around the wood lined walls, advertise drinks at cheap prices. The people packed inside are mainly young. Esther and me qualify as exceptions.

I put my hand flat on the table and I feel the tremor from the loud music. The young people standing near our table edge closer. They obscure the rest of the pub from view. The bruises on my face are bright and they are as large as the fist that caused them. I wish I were sitting in the pub next door, in the darkness of the pokey Coffee House.

'We should be in the Coffee House,' I say.

'So you've said,' says Esther.

'Isaac Newton once visited The Coffee House. Did you know that, Esther? Isaac Newton. Probably stood on the shoulders of others.'

'It's pokey enough.'

'Certainly too pokey for giants,' I say.

'You're an idiot,' says Esther. 'An idiot and a bastard.'

'Every moment is an instant in eternity. Every act is an incident in infinity, something like that. Imagine him next door, wasting the barman's time with information on the gravitational pull of planets.'

I focus on a nearby teenage girl nodding her head. She is either suicidal or ecstatic.

'Isaac became something of a policeman in the end,' I say. 'He finished up working for the *Royal Mint*. He came to Adbury to investigate the production of counterfeit coins.'

'What, like an undercover agent?' says Esther.

'While he was posing as an astronomer? Hardly. Newton hanged twenty-eight people. The sublime intelligence of his generation.'

'As big a bastard as you, then.'

'Isaac enforced the law with gusto, right and wrong.'

'You're more a bastard than an idiot.'

I stand up and fight my way through the crowd. Eventually, I return to the small table. I give Esther a bottle of Budweiser and

I place down a pint of bitter and a double scotch for me. I throw a packet of peanuts at Esther, which she somehow manages to catch.

'What possesses you to pick the noisiest pub in town?' I say.

'Nathan, you're not safe to take to quiet pubs,' says Esther.

I smile and pretend to be full of warm approval. I lean across the glasses on the table and I put my hand under her chin.

'Esther,' I say, 'I have never understood why you are always so attractive when I think you're worthless.'

'I'm dumping you because you're a bastard. I'm sorry about the bruises but it's too little too late.'

Esther leans forward and touches one of the bruises on my face.

'If it was me,' she says, 'I would have thumped Alex back.'

'This is what happens when Alex is riled.' I say.

I swallow half the scotch.

'I never did like putting my tongue in your mouth,' I say.

'Come on, Nathan,' says Esther. 'You never minded putting it anywhere. I don't want to be living like this, Nathan. I want a steady life, somewhere to stay without being hounded. Whatever happens to you, I'll do okay.'

'You don't care.'

'You're a bastard.'

'There is one inside me. It's my sensitivity that helps me recognise him.'

I think about this, the idea almost makes me feel mellow.

'You expect me to somehow survive all this, Esther?' I say.

'I want you to get better but I don't care,' she says. 'You're a bastard, Nathan.'

On the PA system the singer sounds as upset as I feel. I wish Esther did not look so beautiful.

I consider the effort she has made with her appearance. She wears a white skirt, white shoes and a pink off the shoulder sweater with no brassiere underneath and all neatly finished with dark tanned legs. I always imagine the Taylor-Fielder women wearing dark tan stockings the night the bombs had hit Buckland House

'I think I'm finished, Esther,' I say. 'I don't understand why.'

'You're a bastard, and everybody knows,' she says. 'I don't want you to destroy yourself but I don't care. Nathan, ghosts don't go on forever. Not the way you act.'

'Five hundred years old and I never did meet Isaac Newton.'

'You're not just a bastard, you're an idiot.'

'Five hundred years,' I say. 'Of course, I had to sell my soul.'

'If we don't go along with you,' says Esther, 'you get horrible.'

'I like to think I'm horrible as a matter of course.'

Other teenagers fill the space around Esther and me. Before long a teenager brushes against me. I say nothing and let the teenager nod his head through a few bars. I presume the music has bars. The young man wears a red and black lumberjack shirt. I pull the sleeve of his shirt, hard enough for the head of the teenager to come close to mine. The eyes of the teenager are level with those of Esther who smiles hello.

'My guess is you knocked me,' I say.

The teenager speaks to me but looks into the eyes of Esther.

'I'm terribly sorry,' says the teenager. ' It's awfully crowded.'

'We haven't met before?' I say,

I pull the face of the teenager closer.

'In the last couple of hundred years, possibly?' I say.

Esther smiles at the teenager looking into her eyes

'He's messing, love,' says Esther.

The teenager coughs a couple of times. He looks up at his girlfriend who is now standing behind Esther and looking concerned. I pull the teenager even closer. Our faces almost touch. Esther puts her head in her hands. I breathe alcohol all over the face of the teenager.

'I've known vampires,' I say.

I wave a hand to indicate everyone else in the pub.

'A good vampire could suck this lot dry,' I say, 'could go through these well before closing time. Can you imagine afterwards? The heap of drained bodies.'

The girlfriend stands with her mouth open. She is tall, shapeless and thin but the decent human being deep inside me is impressed with her anxiety. The boyfriend has the same nervous quality. I wonder whether the bones of the girlfriend are obvious under the clothes. I let go of the teenager. The table stops the teenager from falling. The teenager moves to join his thin girlfriend. The two of them dig a tunnel through the crowd.

Esther watches them walk away.

'I wouldn't want to be that young again,' she says. 'I never had the nerve to keep men in their place. I was the dope who would say 'Are you fed up with me?' as soon as he looked bored.'

'Not any more,' I say.

'You're different. You're a bastard.'

'God, it is so hot in here. Is it not possible for them to open a window?'

'The doors are open, Nathan.'

I lean back in my chair until my neck rests on top of the chair and I look up at the ceiling. I stare at the loudspeakers that hang from the ceiling.

'They must be playing two records at once,' I say.

'You're off your head,' says Esther.

I stop looking at the two loudspeakers. I watch two blokes approach a girl who is standing by herself. The girl is beautiful, the type of girl it would be hard to imagine ever having hairs on her legs. She has beautiful blonde hair that Esther probably envies.

'Now, she's pretty,' I say

'You'd sleep with her, eh, Nathan?' says Esther.

I take my neck off the back of the chair.

'I would even screw her if she did not have a twat,' I say.

'No you wouldn't, Nathan,' says Esther. 'You wouldn't even talk to her. You're a real bastard.'

I drink the rest of my scotch in one gulp. I lick the taste of the whisky off my teeth. I swallow the remains of the beer. I lower my head close to the debris on the table. I move my head from side to side.

I think about lying next to Kate in her bedroom. I must look crazy, which pleases me.

'Go home, Nathan,' says Esther. 'This was a bad idea. On somebody else the bruises might be impressive. Go pretend you're a ghost somewhere else.'

I say nothing. This encourages Esther.

'I don't begrudge anybody a drink, Nathan,' says Esther, 'but you're a glutton. That's why you read so many books.'

I lift my head from the debris on the table.

'I'm too romantic to be a glutton,' I say. 'You should read . . . Damn, I can't remember. Romantics believe in boundaries, right and wrong.'

'You're a bastard who thinks the rest of us are shite.'

'I am capable of admiration.'

I point at a girl with striped hair.

'See?' I say. ' She's pretty.' I look around for others. 'There are lots, really.'

The music from the loudspeakers is tuneless, as harsh as the chatter and laughter around me.

'I hate the noise people make,' I say. 'They sound like animals feeding. Are those bouncers looking at me?'

'They're just working, Nathan,' says Esther.

'I think they're staring at me.'

I let my face be as vague as possible and I listen to the music again, imagine that by listening I am helping an organ and bass battle through their responsibilities. I listen all the way to the end of the tune.

'I expect I've always hated crowds,' I say.

'I like people,' says Esther.

'You do what they say easily enough.'

'I've known men who were charming.'

'It must have been in your prime.'

'I wanted you to help me stay in Adbury. Without that, all I have is shit.'

I pick up one of the empty beer glasses on the table. I gently lob it into the crowd. I wait for the sound of breaking glass but hear nothing other than music and conversation.

'I wonder if somebody caught it,' I say.

'You make my head ache, Nathan,' says Esther. 'You're too different.'

'Esther, tell me about your tender moments.'

I am not interested in waiting for her reply. I turn around and grin at Mark the barman who smiles at me. Mark wears heavy jewellery around a thick neck. His light T-shirt reveals muscles. I remember admitting to Mark that I was five hundred years old.

I scratch the bruises around my eyes.

'If Mark keeps staring,' I say, ' I'll go and thump him.'

'Nathan, give us a break,' says Esther.

'I never could talk to you for very long.'

'Go talk to one of your mates, then. Sorry, you haven't got any. Nathan, why did you tell the neighbour you just called to screw me?'

'He annoyed me.'

'And I used to think I wasn't worthy of your clever remarks.'

I dismiss Esther with the wave of a hand and I struggle to my feet. I put my hands on the table to stay steady. The people nearby notice that I am having problems. I pick up two empty Budweiser bottles from the table. I turn them upside down over the head of Esther. A couple of drips from the bottles land somewhere on the top of her head. She looks up at the dripping bottles above her head and thinks about a response. She rubs her head to feel if it is really wet.

I place the empty bottles on the table and turn away. I lurch and struggle through the crowd. I hold out my arms in front of my chest like battering rods. I knock a couple of people sideways.

A young man with a small ring through his eyebrow moves to protest.

I raise a fist and say, 'Sonny, I think that facial jewellery is slightly excessive.'

Nobody listens to what I say. My fists are still closed. I stop lurching. I stand in the middle of the crowd and wave my arms around in circles. The crowd moves back to give me some space. I point out Esther for the benefit of everyone. Heads stop nodding, and eyes shift towards where Esther sits. I shout how much I hate her, loud enough for everyone to hear. Behind the bar, Mark interrupts his work to listen. He plays with the heavy jewellery around his neck. The small pieces of chunky metal resemble the granite blocks at Stonehenge. More than a few of the customers are happy to laugh. Esther puts her hands over her eyes. I imagine the hatred underneath her hands.

I lift my arms again and I stagger forwards. When I arrive at the bar, I pretend to throw up over Mark. I grin stupidly, and Mark relaxes a little. I notice Esther stand up and leave the table. She walks past me without stopping

'Nathan, you're being loud,' says Mark. 'No more drink.'

I am aware that other people are listening.

'Nathan, you're a policeman,' says Mark.

'I don't think so,' I say. 'Not really.'

Either side of Mark the barmaids rush around on high heels. Once or twice they glance across at Mark and me.

'You're supposed to set an example, Nathan,' says Mark.

'I don't ever remember reading that,' I say.

'Nathan, Carl was in the other night.'

'Compassionate caring Carl.'

'He asked me to keep an eye out for you. Nathan, you had more sense when you were a kid.'

'So? You didn't always have an earring.'

I lean over the bar, spread my elbows and push others away.

'Mark, did you ever do anything before you were twenty-one?' I say. ' I can't seem to remember.'

One of the barmaids smiles at me as she passes by.

'I'm on my own now,' I say. 'Can I have a beer, Mark?'

'No, you fucking can't.'

'I see. For once in my life I understand perfectly.'

I take my elbows off the table. I stand up straight and yawn, probably because I do not want to be in a trendy pub picked by the woman who has just dumped me. I press my fingers into the edge of the bar. The two young somethings either side of me make sure that they stay out of my reach. The bloke who stands behind me is older rather than young but his hair is loaded with applied gel and he also wears an earring in his right ear. I turn away from the bar and face the bloke with the gel.

'Human, are you?' I say.

The gel allows the hair to pretend it has waves and curls. The T-shirt below the fancy hair says the Mighty Tyrant. The Mighty Tyrant has good white teeth and a tan. He laughs along with his mate who wears a T-shirt that says Angel of Joy. Despite the fact that my face is inches away from them, the two men ignore me. As my arms are no longer resting on the bar, and are available, I rest my hands on the shoulders of the Mighty Tyrant. The Angel of Joy has dry grey hair, no gel and a face that is wider at the bottom than the top. Without moving my head, I look sideways at his mate, the Mighty Tyrant. The Angel of Joy recognises imminent trouble.

I feel like making it really imminent. I grab hold of a selection of gelled curls.

'What on earth have you got on your head?' I say.

'Get your hand off my head,' says the Mighty Tyrant.

'You've got your hand on his head,' says the Angel of Joy. 'Not got enough bruises?'

I believe this remark offensive enough to absolve me of any moral responsibility for what might follow. I turn the Mighty Tyrant around quickly. I have to grip tight to stop my fingers sliding off the gel. I pull the head of the Mighty Tyrant down until it is level with the edge of the bar.

Mark looks down into the eyes of the Mighty Tyrant and struggles to think of something to say. He is better working the till, I think.

I push and rub the face of the Mighty Tyrant against the bar. The nose of the Mighty Tyrant changes shape. From above, the gel is especially noticeable. I see the Angel of Joy looking at Mark critically. Mark manages no more than a nervous smile. He stares down at the eyes of the Mighty Tyrant peeping above the bar. There is a moment of peace, and everything is quiet as decent people hope for the best. Being honest, I find this dull rather than inspirational. I slam the head of the Mighty Tyrant into the bar. The mouth of the Mighty Tyrant fills up with blood. Dental debris falls down his T-shirt. The Mighty Tyrant groans like anyone normal might. The Angel of Joy is too critical and too unhappy to be an Angel of Joy.

I hold on to the head of the Mighty Tyrant and I hear him mumble something to The Angel of Joy at his side.

'Are you all right, Arthur?' says The Angel of Joy.

'No, he's bleeding,' I say. 'He isn't the Mighty Tyrant?'

This is a realisation I find to be encouraging. I slam the head I am holding back into the bar. More blood spills from the mouth of Arthur. His knees buckle. Mark can no longer see the eyes peeping above the bar and he becomes anxious. I keep hold of the head but let the knees sink to the floor.

The Angel of Joy breathes anxiously. He looks around for possible friends but nobody responds. I let go of the gelled hair and wipe my hands on the T-shirt of the Angel of Joy. While Arthur, the Mighty Tyrant, rests on his knees, he bends his head and puts his hands to his face. He searches for the gaps in his teeth with his tongue. The movement of his face makes me think of the baby in the gymnasium.

'Oh, no,' says Arthur, the Mighty Tyrant, and more blood leaves his mouth.

The Angel of Joy steps forward to put his arms around the shoulders of his friend.

'What do I tell the wife?' says Arthur, the Mighty Tyrant.

He mumbles the words into his hands. The Angel of Joy points a finger at me.

'Happy?' says the Angel of Joy.

'I know it's not fashionable,' I say, 'but there are people who think violence can be a route to self-discovery.'

I grin and wink.

'You destructive lunatic,' says the Angel of Joy.

Just as I am anticipating my being victorious in an interesting existential argument, the bouncers arrive. They are breathless, and the resentment on their faces is obvious. Both bouncers are taller and heavier than me. Who cares, I think. They both wear short leather jackets over T-shirts with green onions embroidered on the chest. The elder bouncer has an especially clean bald head. The younger has hair.

'Outside,' says the bouncer with the bald head.

'A superior gorilla,' I explain to a nearby spectator. 'It's why he doesn't have hair.'

This theory is less convincing than the previous existentialism, I realise. Maybe I am like Mark and better as a man of action. The nearby spectator is female. She stands with her legs close together and with her mouth open. I steal her beer bottle before she is able to close her mouth.

'Put the bottle down, sir,' says the bouncer with hair.

'Outside,' says the bouncer with the clean bald head.

The bouncer with the hair pretends to be patient.

'Please, sir,' he says. 'We're trying to help. Put the bottle down.'

'Certainly,' I say.

I thump the middle of the bald head with the bottle. The truth is I am curious as to what will happen. I hear a decent thud but the bottle does not break.

'I find shiny heads impossible to resist,' I say.

This is only half true.

The bouncer with the bald head tries to stare up through his brain. His eyes trace two lines to a single point on top of his shiny head.

'That's going to bruise,' he says.

'Shouldn't you be feeling faint?' I say.

'I'll have to wear a cap. I look daft in a cap.'

'You must be a drum or something.'

'It's actually quite painful, sir.'

'Trev was once hit with an iron bar,' says the bouncer with hair.

Trev holds out his hand for me to give him the bottle.

'Put the bottle down, sir,' he says.

Trev has no desire to remember the iron bar, I reckon.

I swing the bottle wildly. The bouncers stop edging forward. The crowd in the pub no longer makes a noise. The music continues but nobody notices and it sounds quieter. Behind the bouncer, and unnoticed by most, the Angel of Joy lifts Arthur to his feet. Arthur is still bleeding from his mouth. I would like to help but I have other issues. Instead, I keep swinging the bottle. I catch the chin of the bouncer with hair. The glass bottle on his jaw produces a sharp noise, nothing like a thud. The expression above the chin definitely changes.

'Now, listen, you,' says the bouncer with the hair.

I recognise this as moral disapproval.

I move nearer to the bouncers. The two men have been trained, and I know their competence from experience. They evaluate the situation and realise that I am a mistake of a human being that needs his head kicking in. I no longer care, as an epitaph it is quite acceptable. The bouncers jump me and thump and kick. They keep calling me a bastard. I keep swinging the bottle. I lash out with my feet. As I fall to the floor, I am aware that more than the bouncers think I am a mistake of a human being. I spit out at whoever is near. Behind me, it is quiet. I assume Mark is watching. The high heels of the barmaids sound at rest, so the barmaids are presumably doing the same. The two bouncers swing their fists. Other people pile into the scuffle. I kick out the best I can and attempt to hit anyone who comes close. The two bouncers thump whoever is near them. It has become complicated. Some of the others throw punches at the bouncers, and some of the people who hit me are content to hit other people who, if hit, usually respond by hitting someone else again. In the end the bouncers are happy to hit anyone, and everyone else is happy to do the same. More people join me on the floor.

The police arrive while the majority of the crowd is still standing. The police have truncheons and they hit people with just as much enthusiasm as anyone else. The bodies pile up around me. I wonder what ever happened to the Mighty Tyrant and the Angel of Joy. The sergeant in charge lets his team sort out the bodies into those who need medical treatment and those who do not. Those who do are left lying and sitting on the floor. The police place the others in a line in front of the bar and tell them to shut up. One young man protests that he is innocent, and a policeman hits him with a truncheon. Inevitably, I am having regrets. The police put the young man alongside the others needing medical treatment lying on the floor. I am dug out from the pile of suffering bodies.

At the bar a fit young policeman inspects the bald head of the bouncer for a possible bruise. Mark stands alone and rehearses denying responsibility. I am the first to be taken away to the cells. I am charged with causing an affray and making an assault occasioning actual bodily harm. All this has been quite demanding, I need a drink and to relax.

2 2

NATHAN IS RESTING

Somebody needs to tell me where the hell I am. My eyes are closed but I am too weary to open them. I am also afraid, really afraid. I feel very different from how I felt in the Green Onion. Then self-destruction was tempting and appeared possible but even that hope has drifted away from me. I am wrapped tight inside a bed and feel like someone who is having every one of their moments prescribed by something impossible to reach. But, providing I tell myself not to care, I should be able to float towards pain free nothing. I have had the strangest dreams, as if I was back on the smack that they had pumped into me all those years ago. I also dreamt that I was being tortured again. This particular dream is never fun but this time I was more terrified than when it actually happened because, as terrible as the dreams and the violence always are, this time they were sustained by a relentless conviction that it would happen again and again. I am miserable but feel as high as a kite. What is the matter with me? What am I supposed to do?

A voice says, 'Nathan, what did you do?'

I keep my eyes closed. Behind me, there are large pillows. I am in pain but my body is comfortable. I am tempted to think that Kate has visited and propped pillows behind my head again.

'Nathan, are you awake?' says the voice.

'No,' I say.

The person with the voice laughs.

'Why don't you open your eyes?' says the voice.

'I am asleep,' I say.

The person with the voice laughs again.

'Are your eyes sore?' says the voice.

I am not sure, I think. Behind the eyelids, I see fractures of coloured light that remind me of pins and needles. Whether the fractures are actually causing pain, I do not know. They make me think of pain.

'Nathan, what did you do last night?' says the voice.

I realise that I am talking to Carl and I open my eyes. He is sitting in an armchair and he is next to my bed.

'I was drunk and I had a fight,' I say. 'I was arrested and I have been charged. I am in trouble, Carl.'

He is wearing his uniform. I rarely see him when he is not. Carl has had a haircut. It is easy to notice because the milk coloured streaks always change places afterwards. His face is red and cheerless.

'The Incident Unit wants to interview you, Nathan,' says Carl.

'I've already been charged,' I say. 'Can I go to sleep again?'

The room is not my own. I am lying in a tall high bed with very clean sheets. The walls are covered with paint as clean as the sheets. There is the usual hospital stuff either side of the bed.

'Why am I in hospital?' I say.

'Because I fiddled it,' says Carl.

I am confused and I say nothing.

'I am a true friend,' says Carl.

Neither of us says anything. I look around the room but there is little to see, a TV on the wall and a glass of water within my reach. I can hear nothing outside, none of the bustle in the hospital that must exist elsewhere. Carl sighs a couple of times. He crosses his legs.

Eventually, he speaks, 'Esther is dead.'

I close my eyes and I think about the horrific dreams of the night. Esther is dead, and I imagine her suffering more than I did. I am not sure if I feel grief or not. I am shocked but weirdly I feel upstaged. Nothing puts you in your place like the death of someone else. Well, there is something but that is just as trivial as the rest.

The plain hospital room makes suggestions to my wandering mind, nothing sensible, no more than modest mystery in a quiet room. The gap between sleep and being awake feels enormous.

'Esther is dead,' I say.

'You should be in the station being interviewed,' says Carl. 'As soon as I got wind, I rushed you here and persuaded Dr Long to sign a statement saying that you needed urgent treatment.'

'You shouldn't have.'

'I have a sense of responsibility. You don't have any at all, do you, Nathan?'

'Esther shouldn't be dead. She had a business to run.'

'All the people I expected to look after me when I was young I am now watching out for, you and mother. There are others as well.'

'Everybody thought Esther was gorgeous.'

'She isn't any more.'

'She shouldn't be dead.'

'I shouldn't be responsible Detective Superintendent Carl Hart but I am, and you shouldn't be a forty year old fucking idiot but you are.'

I think about the question that I am afraid of asking. I remember the insults in the pub but I had insulted Esther before. She was gorgeous, my insults she could treat with contempt.

'Nathan,' says Carl, 'you're so terrified of responsibility you'd rather destroy yourself. I don't get that. What must your kids think of you?'

'Not much,' I say.

'You and Esther thought I was frightened of McGrath,' says Carl.

Every time I think of Esther, I remember her being angry.

'It suited me,' says Carl. 'I could have sorted McGrath. It suited me, and it was best for Adbury. I never did take to Esther.'

'She shouldn't be dead,' I say.

'Kate hasn't left. She's in the station looking at her report again.'

'She isn't worried about me, then?'

Carl laughs.

'Kate looks out for Kate,' he says. 'Now Esther is dead, she'll be adding some weight to what she has written. A couple of interviews and a few hundred words, and she's been here almost a week.'

'She's entitled to take a holiday,' I say.

'Holiday one day and work the next, it doesn't feel right to me. What would have happened if she'd been back in Liverpool? She'd have put in the memory stick and typed. She wouldn't have popped into the station.'

'Well, if she is still here.'

'I want her to go back to Liverpool. She shouldn't be dipping in and out like this. I don't mind anybody staying the course but not work one day and holiday the next. The nurses don't come in much, do they?'

'I haven't had an operation, I suppose.'

'When all this is over, I hope people realise I stayed the course. I am there at home with my mother and I am here with you and I talk to McGrath so he is responsible. Kate came to see me this morning. She was going on about McGrath. She said I'd forgotten how to be a real copper. I've done what's best for Adbury. Kate talks to me about how I should be. I've stayed the course. Kate fucked off to Liverpool.'

Another day and I would have argued, said something about obligation and how some should stay the course and others should move around. What was important was to know what you did best. I remembered Esther talking about wanting a man who would help her stay. I should have said something but what I thought took an awfully long time to arrive.

'I've lost a stone, you know,' says Carl. 'Nothing looks worse than a too tight uniform. I'll see that through to the end as well.'

I know why I did not ask the question I wanted to ask earlier. I wanted to believe that Esther had simply disappeared into nothing and that without too much effort I could do the same. Now, I have to ask the question.

'How did Esther die?' I say.

'She was killed,' says Carl.

'By McGrath?'

'He has an alibi. You're the main suspect, Nathan. The Major Incident Unit will only wait for so long. I have told them that a confession from a man under psychiatric treatment will be worthless but that will only work for today. What happened last night, Nathan?'

'I caught a taxi home after I was charged.'

'The desk sergeant said you were still pissed.'

'I went home in a taxi.'

'The Major Incident Unit have found the taxi driver. What happened after that at home?'

'I had a drink.'

'You had another drink?'

'I was still standing, so I thought why not. I must have collapsed. I woke up here.'

'I found you asleep in bed. I called Dr Long, and we brought you here.'

'I do not remember any of that.'

'Esther told Kate in her interview that you were back on the smack.'

'No, I told Esther that I bought it to keep the temptation at bay. It is easier not to take it when you know it is there. I have discussed this with Dr Long.'

'Esther told Kate. You have had tests in here, Nathan. They found all sorts in your bloodstream. Alcohol, sleeping pills and heroin.'

'I don't take sleeping pills,' I say. 'I'm not back on the smack. I was hammered with the booze. I went home in the taxi, drank some whisky and collapsed on the couch. After that, I do not remember.'

'This is not a good start, Nathan,' says Carl.

'I was asleep.'

'You wanted to fight the world last night, Nathan. As Kate would say, you are a very believable suspect.'

If only I could disappear, all of me and from myself. I no longer resented Esther upstaging me with her death. I envied her the nothing.

'The killing of Esther was not an accident,' says Carl. 'The crime was particularly violent. There is bad bruising around her neck, and she suffered heavy blows to her head.'

'I have never assaulted Esther, ever,' I say.

'You were thumping complete strangers last night. Kate thinks you're a pathetic mess. I've spoken to the Major Incident people. Photographs of Buckland House were left all over Esther.'

'There are some in her house, I think.'

'And who would know what they meant?' says Carl.

'This is McGrath,' I say. 'He has set me up. We've been doing deals with a murderer.'

'We didn't do deals, Nathan. I put pressure on McGrath so he acted responsibly.'

I am thinking about the heroin that is in my body. God, I was drunk when I arrived home. The whisky may have sent me over the edge. If only I could remember.

'McGrath sells dope,' I say.

'Not in the schools or on the streets; the pubs and the clubs, that's all. In his own way, McGrath has stayed the course.'

I find it surprisingly easy to lie there and imagine what might follow, being interviewed, charged with murder and then sentenced. I would finally leave Adbury. With the help of Dr Long, I might be sentenced to psychiatric treatment in a secure establishment. No responsibility in there to avoid, I think. It is still a future, though, that has to be faced, no disappearing away from myself inside those places. I am relaxed but afraid, very afraid.

2 3

NATHAN OUTSIDE HIS HOSPITAL ROOM

I am standing in another damned doorway. The door opens to a hospital corridor. I am washed, shaved and dressed. Dr Long told me just before midnight that the Major Incident Unit intended to visit. I have decided not to wait. I know the two people who are in the corridor. Rena is the policewoman who first visited Esther to look at the yellow paint. She sits close to the door that opens to outside. I know little about her except that she has always indulged me with a smile in the station. She is in her mid-twenties. Carl thinks that she has career potential. Close to the door to my room sits the nurse, Jim Senior. Jim is tall, plain and bald. He looks tired. He exists as a warning against old age. He has already visited me several times since my arrival but I also know him from my previous visits to Dr Long. We should all be friends, really, but they are not pleased to see me.

'Not interested in the TV, are we?' says Jim.

This is a calculated remark to keep me at bay. Rena and Jim are irritated by my presence. Jim puts down on the chair next to him the magazine he has been reading. The cover has a photograph of a couple of movie stars. Jim and Rena exchange concerned glances.

'You could have waited until I'd had my smoking break,' says Jim.

I know from his earlier visits to my room that Jim likes to make a light-hearted remark whatever the circumstances. I stay in the doorway and face Rena, Jim and the corridor. Rena stands up and leans against a wall. Rena smiles, leaves the wall and stands with her legs apart like someone ready for action. These two do not worry me, I think. I look again at the photograph of the beautiful movie stars.

'Esther should not be dead,' I say.

Rena and Jim say nothing, glance at one another again. Jim looks even more serious and caring than normal. Rena looks worried.

'Do you want something to read?' says Jim. 'I really think you should go back to bed, Nathan.'

'I like to read myself,' says Rena and she adds a false smile.

I remember helping Rena with the report she wrote after visiting Esther. My decline has been fast, and I would like it to be over.

'You must get bored in there,' says Jim.

He points at me but he is indicating the room.

'Nothing to do?' says Jim.

'The nothing isn't there,' I say.

Rena and Jim look at one another again with the same concerned glances. Rena raises her eyebrows. If she does that again, I will smack her in the face, I think.

'I should be in a rehab' unit,' I say. 'If I have a relapse, you wouldn't know how to look after me.'

Jim stands up. The two are now leaning against the same wall opposite my room. Jim looks earnest, and Rena is still worried.

'You're bound to be edgy, Nathan,' says Jim. 'I'll get you some more books tomorrow.'

Jim points away from outside and towards the PC at the end of the corridor.

'We can go on Amazon on the machine,' says Jim. 'Me and you.'

'I feel like I've lived a life in there,' I say.

I lean against a doorframe, much like I did when I saw Carl in the hotel.

'Me, I like working slow nights,' says Jim.

The tone of his voice changes to something stern.

'Me,' he says, 'I like the patients all peaceful.'

Rena is still staring at me. Her eyebrows are where they should be but she now has a stupid smile. I am just as happy to smack the smile as the eyebrow.

'I've been watching television,' I say. 'It must make you feel light-headed. I probably need a good meal inside me.'

Rena and Jim move silently and slowly along the wall towards each other. They must think that I am stupid. Why not, I think, they are entitled. When they are standing close to one another, they step forward so they are not leaning against the wall.

'I'm not going back in there,' I say.

'People are coming to see you tomorrow, Nathan,' says Jim, 'it won't be as dull.'

'It is not dull enough,' I say. 'There's nowhere empty to float to.'

I think of Esther lost in nothing but I have been doing that all day. Jim is much taller than Rena who is almost petite. I think it would be no bad idea if Rena said something helpful. The wary expression on her face makes it clear that she is unlikely to speak soon.

'We should have taken your clothes away,' says Jim.

I smile wide enough to show all my teeth. I feel capable of disturbing people with a smile.

'Are you pretending to be crazy for later?' says Jim.

'Like Hamlet, you mean?' I say.

I cross my arms and breathe through my nostrils. It probably feels more impressive than it looks.

'I'm not standing here all night,' I say.

'Sorry if we're boring you,' says Rena.

Silly eyebrows, stupid smile and sarcastic remark, I think. This is a woman I can easily introduce to the abyss.

'How on earth did you get out of your room?' says Jim.

'I concentrated really hard,' I say.

'You look like a ghost out of the past.'

Jim is more perceptive than I realised.

'The TV makes my head feel strange,' I say.

'You look strange.'

'The TV is all rubbish anyway. You don't realise at home because of DVDs.'

I produce my wide smile again. This worries Rena.

'Nathan, go and lie down,' says Jim, 'or I'll arrange for you to be taken into police custody right now. You wouldn't want that, Nathan. Me, neither.'

'Dr Long has promised me twenty four hours leave,' I say.

'Oh, yeah?' says Rena.

After the silence the unpleasant tone in her voice is a surprise.

'All this is extremely serious,' says Jim.

'I know it's serious,' I say. 'It's really serious, too serious for me to stay. Esther should not be dead.'

'Now, Nathan, you don't want to get me into trouble with Dr Long.'

'She always forgives me. You won't be as big a disappointment to her as I am.'

Jim ponders on this helpful remark of mine, maybe it will help him with his future, I think.

'I was reading about Nicole Kidman before you came out of your room,' says Jim.

This does not sound like a man thinking about his future. My helpful remark has not helped Jim in the way I had hoped.

'Do us a favour, Nathan,' says Jim. 'Take off the clothes and go to bed.'

Rena smiles and this time she raises an eyebrow at me.

'The bombs are to be dropped on Buckland House tonight,' I say.

'Oh, Jesus,' says Rena.

'I'll make us all a cup of tea,' says Jim.

'I want to go outside,' I say.

The light in the narrow corridor is bright and warm. I am too old and tired to be standing in a bright light, I think.

'I'm tired of being cooped up,' I say.

'Nathan,' says Jim, 'you are clearly upset. Rest is as good as it gets, Nathan.'

'I don't want to be Nathan anymore.'

This remark perplexes Rena. She is a young girl with a fresh complexion. I doubt if she deserves my rubbish. She raises an eyebrow, and my sympathy disappears.

'I've made my mind up,' I say. 'I want to go and meet people.'

'He's taking the piss,' says Rena.

Wait until I really start, I think.

'Leave it to me,' says Jim. 'We'll all go out tomorrow.'

'I want to go out now,' I say.

Jim is trying to be constructive. I am too easily prone to be contemptuous, I suppose.

'No, Nathan,' says Rena. 'No chance.'

'If either of you attempt to prevent me from leaving,' I say, 'I will not hesitate to use violence.'

'Not either, Nathan, both of us, right, Jim?' says Nena.

'Nathan wouldn't hurt me,' says Jim. 'Nathan, I'm medical staff. We're trying to look after you.'

'Jim,' I say, 'I have the responsibilities of a guardian angel. I have been asleep for over fifty years.'

'Oh, Jesus,' says Rena.

Inevitably, the unpleasant tone returns to her voice.

'Eight hours sleep actually,' says Jim, 'still, a long time. I'll go make a cup of tea. A cup of tea will make you feel better.'

'I really do have to walk straight out of here,' I say.

'I've swopped a shift, Nathan. This isn't fair on me.'

Oddly, this instance of self-pity in Jim does not surprise me. The constant light-hearted remarks he has made in my room had already made me suspicious.

'Neither of you qualifies for a guardian angel just yet,' I say.

'Oh, shut up, Nathan,' says Rena.

Jim steps forward and puts his arm around my shoulder.

'Nathan,' he says, 'I'm sorry I'm not a guardian angel.'

For somebody like Jim, this may be true.

'And you're better off not being one,' says Jim.

'I don't want to be Nathan,' I say.

'He's fucking gone,' says Rena.

She should really say nothing, even if she does have destructive eyebrows. Jim puts both his hands on my shoulders.

'Nathan,' he says, 'you're supposed to be under observation.'

'Jim, you look very tired,' I say.

'We're all tired. I'll have to phone.'

He lifts his hands away from my shoulders.

'If we get some fresh air,' I say.

'Spare us,' says Rena.

Jim turns to Rena.

'Phone her,' says Jim. 'Tell Dr Long he's left.'

'I don't have to go straight away,' I say.

'Oh, go,' says Rena. 'Nathan, you're not a guardian angel.'

'Rena, don't upset him,' says Jim. 'Let him be a guardian angel if that's what he wants to be.'

'He's round the fucking bend,' says Rena.

'I can't be,' I say. 'None of us flip just like that.'

'Nathan, go and lie down and sleep,' says Jim.

'I've just slept for fifty years.'

'Jim will make you a cup of tea,' says Rena. 'Nathan, don't make me make a phone call.'

'The doctor will be here soon enough,' says Jim.

Rena pulls the mobile phone off her belt.

'I'm tired of this,' she says. 'I'll phone.'

Jim and me watch Rena dial. She puts the phone back on her belt.

'I never have a signal this time of day,' she says.

I say nothing.

'This is going to end badly,' says Rena.

Bingo, Rena makes a sensible remark. Jim walks up and down the corridor. He stops and rubs his eyes until they are red and watery. He turns and stands next to me.

'We can use Dr Long's phone,' he says.

I have forgotten why we want to make a phone call.

'No,' I say, 'a guardian angel needs someone to guard.'

'Nathan, that's not what people want,' says Rena. 'They want to be left alone.'

When she is not raising an eyebrow or needing help with an incident report, Rena can be quite opinionated. Jim shuffles around in the corridor before moving closer to Rena.

'I've got to go,' I say. 'If I stay here any longer, I'll go crazy.'

'You are crazy, you fucking idiot,' says Rena.

Obviously, I find the remark objectionable, and that is apart from the history of raised eyebrows and sarcastic smiles. My right uppercut lifts Jim off the floor. His neck makes a horrible noise immediately. Jim lands on the floor a little later. His eyes close, and he falls asleep. Rena steps forward to protest. I spot the fillings at the back of her open mouth and I butt her in the face. She steps back and holds her bleeding nose with her two hands. She steps over Jim and sits down on the chair opposite my room.

'I think my nose is broken,' she says.

The words inside the blood sound like a cough. On the floor, Jim groans and suffers but manages an acceptable snore.

'Get out, Nathan,' says Rena.

She is holding her nose and she is tearful but not hysterical.

'I'll get you something to stop the blood,' I say.

'Nathan, get out,' says Rena.

'The Police Federation will pay for plastic surgery.'

'Nathan, get out.'

A good plastic surgeon might improve her profile, I think. This thought I keep to myself.

I walk around Jim and past Rena. I step into the dark outside and feel comfortable. I think about Jim unconscious on the floor and Rena with her broken nose although it may not even be broken. It did bleed a lot, though. Well, you do not get to hell without breaking a few eggs.

2 4

NATHAN IN A LARGE AND POPULOUS SETTLEMENT

I have arrived in the city of Chester. It has been difficult during the morning hours of darkness or *madrugada*, as the Spanish would say. My house was without a police presence when I called, so Jim and Rena must have argued before making a decision, or maybe they wanted to suffer for a few moments. Anyway, I am here and I have a car, a gun but not enough money. I am doomed but free. The doom I could do without if I am honest but the free I could get used to.

'Big Issue,' says a young man standing near me. 'Help the homeless.'

The morning is dry and all right. Good weather for selling copies of the *Big Issue*, I would think. The young man shouting Big Issue is tall, overweight and untidily dressed in well-worn jeans and trainers. His long straight hair lays flat against his head. His face is unshaved and the stubble neatly dodges the occasional pimple. We are both standing in front of the Pizza Hut restaurant in Chester and right next to the giant advertisement for the all you can eat special. Inside the Pizza Hut a young couple stare at the young man, who is called T Bone, and me. Outside, an old lady inspects the name and photograph on the *Big Issue* ID badge. I watch the old lady pay the money to T Bone and refuse a *Big Issue*. Two schoolgirls explain that they are unable to afford the magazine.

'Big Issue, help the homeless,' says T Bone.

'Guardian Angels,' I say. 'Help us help others.'

T Bone lifts his unshaved face. He sticks out his chin and narrows his eyes.

'Money for guarding susceptible souls,' I say.

'I don't fucking need this,' T Bone says this quietly. Not as loud as *Big Issue* help the homeless.

T Bone mumbles something about unfairness.

Two pretty girls stop to talk and laugh before dropping a pound into the can I have put on the pavement in front of me. Why am I doing this?

The idea occurred to me as I was watching T Bone. I thought it might lead to something. I might earn some extra money, and who will be looking for me amongst invisible *Big Issue* salesmen. But this is only rationalisation. Something in me fancies doing it, and I have no illusions that I will be free for long. It is crazy and daft but it suits my mood. Maybe this will sweeten the doom. I have become a guardian angel rather easily. The coin rolls around the can echoing the laughter from the girls. The can props up my crudely written sign that says, 'Donations needed to see souls through eternity.' The girls have clean hair, good faces, decent jeans and great figures. I try and act as if I am supposed to be normal.

'Help guardian angels be strong enough to guard,' I say. 'Lost souls need your help.'

'Aren't you a bit old?' says T Bone.

'I don't age. I'm immortal.'

'This is my pitch. What the fuck you up to?'

I say nothing and point at what is written on the card.

'It's always been my pitch,' says T Bone. 'I'm not standing for this. I don't stand for Peruvian pipe players. I don't stand for you.'

I try to speak like I imagine a guardian angel might.

'I am not welcome?' I say.

I sound more like Bela Lugosi, the movie vampire.

'You taking the piss?' says T Bone.

'Actually, I've had nothing to eat today,' I say.

I cannot get that damned Bela Lugosi accent out of my head.

I remember Esther not being able to hear her own voice and how little sympathy I had for her trips to Dr Long. Esther should not be dead, and I have to stop talking like Bela Lugosi.

'You want to know my secrets?' I say.

More Bela Lugosi, I am afraid.

'He's coming it,' says T Bone to no one in particular.

Chester is busy with shoppers and tourists. I pose for those who stop to listen and I look at my can and scruffy card. A couple of Japanese wearing checked trousers smile at each other and then me. One of them throws a two-pound coin. The coin rings as soon as it lands in the can.

'This makes me see my arse,' says T Bone. 'Him fucking coming here and stealing my patch.'

'I haven't eaten since yesterday,' I say. 'I'm somewhat preoccupied with my appetite at the moment.'

Indeed, this emphasis on practicalities has helped me stop talking like Bela Lugosi.

'Eat?' says T Bone. 'You said you were fucking immortal.'

'I can take you to a tomb where my name is written for all to see,' I say.

'You're a fucking lunatic.'

Wherever I go in Cheshire, the opinion about me is consistent. The shoppers around T Bone wait for me to respond.

'You don't understand,' I say. 'I'm from another world.'

'Oh, yeah,' says T Bone. 'Well, you've made a big mistake coming to this one.'

'My destiny has brought me here,' I say.

'Your what?'

T Bone looks at the watching shoppers to see what they think. Nobody indicates that they believe he might be talking to a lunatic. I feel that this is progress, which is probably why I have the confidence to say what I say next.

'I have an unfulfilled destiny,' I say. 'I'm passing through.'

'I've never heard so much shite,' says T Bone,

I lean forward and I pull T Bone towards me by his *Big Issue* registration badge. In the photograph, T Bone has a beard and dyed blonde streaks in his hair, which makes me think of the more authentic appearance of Carl. All that seems an age away. I let go of the badge.

'T Bone?' I say.

'T Bone Rogers,' says T Bone.

'But why T Bone?'

'I'm an authorised vendor.'

'Then go ahead and vend, T Bone.'

'You're coming it again.'

I hear the shoppers take sides amongst themselves. Half believe in the principle of registration badges while others disapprove of the manner of T Bone. I am definitely the more polite.

'I have a suspicion you don't even sleep on the streets,' I say.

T Bone lifts up his registration badge so he can see it himself.

'I don't have to sleep on the fucking streets,' says T Bone.

This idea shocks some of the shoppers more than the language of T Bone. He looks down at the pavement. We hear the shoppers express doubts about his right to sell the *Big Issue*.

'I've just found temporary accommodation,' says T Bone.

'Perhaps,' I say and I smile with the sarcastic smile I remember on the face of Rena.

I hope the smile of Rena will not haunt me like the voice of Bela Lugosi. Deliberately, I become stern.

'Drugs was it?' I say.

'Drugs it is,' says T Bone.

We both look around and realise that there is a crowd watching. T Bone explains for their benefit.

'I'm making progress,' he says.

I feel I should be sympathetic, even if he is an aggressive competitor.

'T Bone,' I say, 'some of us can't make it on our own.'

Within the crowd a small group of sun-tanned middle-aged women applaud.

I am beginning to feel friendly towards T Bone. The stubble on his pale face and his untidy clothes add to an obvious lack of charm but his pimples will have unpleasant memories.

'T Bone,' I say, 'even the greatest of the guardian angels who have been wandering amongst strangers for generations have had to occasionally pause for company.'

'I'm not sure if that is true,' says an anonymous voice in the crowd.

A couple of watching shoppers drift away. I watch a woman in expensive clothes make her way through the thinning crowd. The woman in expensive clothes helps the crowd thin more. Her expensive clothes remind me of Kate.

'T Bone,' I say, 'I've journeyed a long way to talk to you.'

'You're trying to scrounge a few bob for a pizza,' says T Bone.

'Think of the damage drugs do to you.'

Nobody applauds but I hear murmurs of support.

'I don't talk about drugs,' says T Bone.

A man in a grey business suit and shiny shoes stops walking and joins the crowd. He stands next to T Bone. The man in a grey business suit tries to read the cover of the *Big Issue*. He wears a white shirt and bright tie. He has short dark hair and a middle-aged face that implies fitness and well being. He is the type of man whom I have imagined I could have been. T Bone is less impressed.

'Well, Arsehole?' he says.

'This is T Bone,' I say.

'I was thinking of buying a *Big Issue*,' says the man in the suit previously identified by T Bone as Arsehole.

'Did I say Big Issue, help the homeless?' says T Bone.

'I must have assumed you did,' says the man in the suit previously identified by T Bone as Arsehole.

T Bone turns and faces me.

'Did I say *Big Issue* help the homeless?' he says.

'I wasn't listening,' I say. 'I was worrying about eternity. The paradise of the infinite.'

T Bone becomes quiet. He does not look as if he is thinking about infinity.

'It says you're an authorised vendor,' says the man in the suit previously identified as you know what.

'Do I look like I'm fucking vending?' says T Bone.

'They're having an argument,' someone shouts.

The crowd is reduced. If T Bone had ever been thinking about the infinite, he has definitely moved on.

'Like what is your problem, pal?' says T Bone.

'It changes from day to day,' says the man in the suit.

'I was having an argument with him.'

T Bone points at me. I point at myself, willing, as always, to aid clarification. The smart man in the suit looks at my tin and the card with the sign.

'No way is he an immortal,' says T Bone. 'Immortals don't need to fucking eat like he does.'

'He's right and he isn't,' I say.

'Wanting to be a guardian angel is extremely positive,' says the man in the suit.

I regard this as a compliment and I acknowledge receipt with a self-effacing smile.

'Fuck off, will you, eh?' says T Bone. 'Don't you get asked enough to buy *Big Issues*?'

The man in the suit speaks with an education polished baritone, warm chocolate.

'I just want a reason not to buy another,' he says.

'T Bone is just argumentative,' I say. 'Give him a Big Issue, T Bone.'

'No,' says T Bone. 'I don't want to. I sell Big Issues when I say and providing that I'm not otherwise engaged with fucking nut cases that think they are immortal guardian angels.'

'Of all the street corners in all the towns a guardian angel can pick I had to pick this one,' I say.

NATHAN IN A LARGE AND POPULOUS SETTLEMENT

A couple of people in the crowd recognise the quote and giggle.

The man in the suit speaks to me, 'Would you like the money instead?'

'Tell him to fuck off,' says T Bone.

The man straightens his bright tie. The chocolate voice becomes more like crispy biscuit.

'I'm not fucking anywhere,' he says.

'He's a nark,' says T Bone. 'He thinks you're fucking immortal.'

Nobody is leaving the crowd. Since the well-dressed woman walked through, the crowd has grown again. The man in the suit bends forward and reads the details on the registration badge of T Bone. His voice melts enough for fruit and nut to appear in the chocolate.

'Have you two any idea how many times I've been asked to buy a *Big Issue* in the last twelve months?' he says. 'How many manipulative appeals I endure, and the number of occasions that guilt and personal responsibility has been implied?'

'At least, I'm not fucking immortal,' says T Bone.

'T Bone's too direct to be manipulative,' I say. 'I'm his guardian angel.'

'Like fuck he is. I'm going to get a policeman.'

The man in the suit waves his hand.

'Why are *Big Issue* sellers mainly men?' he says

'We must be more idealistic,' I say.

'It's no job for a woman,' says T Bone.

'I pass six *Big Issues* sellers every lunch hour,' says the man. 'I can't buy six every day.'

T Bone looks up and down the street.

'I can't see a copper anywhere,' he says. 'This isn't fucking law and order, is it?'

'I'm obliged to say no twenty nine times a week,' says the man. 'Twenty nine times I'm looked at as if I'm the lowest specimen on the planet.'

'We're trained not to do that,' says T Bone.

'Six times five minus one,' I explain.

I use my fingers to make the concept simple.

'I can fucking add up,' says T Bone.

'Multiplication, actually,' I say.

'That takes no account of weekends when I'm with my family,' says the man in the suit.

'What about holidays?' says T Bone.

'They balance out weekends. Let's call it a minimum of twenty nine times fifty two.'

'I'd say total. No fucking way is it minimum.'

I say nothing but I am inclined to concede that T Bone may have a point. Of course, being his guardian angel may mean that I am biased.

'Fifty two multiplied by twenty nine equals fifteen hundred and eight,' says the man in the suit.

'We don't need you walking around counting *Big Issue* sellers and fucking multiplying,' says T Bone.

'He thinks he can survive without people,' I say.

I point at T Bone but am in no way judgemental. I am aware of my responsibilities as a guardian angel.

'Ah, one of those,' says the man in the suit.

The wrinkles in his brow are deep enough to trap flies. The crowd edges back from the argument but it still watches and listens.

'He says he buys one every week,' says T Bone. 'We don't know he does.'

'Twenty nine times every week for two years,' says the man.

'Three thousand and sixteen,' I say. 'It's horrible remembering when we can multiply.'

'What the fuck does that mean?' says T Bone.

'I understand what he means,' says the man.

This surprises me because I felt a little unsure as I said it. I see a policewoman appear at the end of the street. She wears a yellow waterproof slip over her uniform. I remember being young and in uniform, being a vague relative to what I am now. I step back, stand close to a shop window. There are shoppers ahead of T Bone, the man in the suit and me. They walk towards the policewoman.

Her presence makes me wary, and T Bone notices the change in me. His eyes track back along the street towards the policewoman.

'Don't call her,' I say.

'For a teapot, he's soft on the right side,' says T Bone.

'Don't call him a teapot,' says the man in the suit.

I pick up my can of coins. The policewoman walks along the street towards us. The remaining shoppers form a circle around T Bone, the man in the suit and me. They leave a gap for the policewoman to walk through. The policewoman is young and smiles at as many people as she can. She rests hands on stocky hips. She looks at me as if I am the most suspicious. Of course, I am not the authorised vendor.

'What about you, Sunshine?' says the policewoman.

'I'm leaving Chester,' says Sunshine, who is me. 'I've got to see my sister. I'm trying to raise my train fare.'

'I might be daft enough to believe you if you start walking.'

The shoppers and tourists who are watching T Bone and me are inspired by this and they begin to leave.

'I'm on my lunch hour,' says the man in the suit. 'I own a large building store nearby, close to the river.'

The policewoman smiles at the man in the suit. She likes his voice, I think.

'It might be best if you all took a lunch hour,' says the policewoman.

'I was going back to work,' says the man in the suit.

The policewoman reads the *Big Issue* authorisation badge.

'What about you, T Bone?' she says, as if he is not the first T Bone she has met in Chester.

'I'm going for fish and chips,' says T Bone.

T Bone clutches his *Big Issue* editions to his chest. As a man ready to search for fish and chips, he is believable.

'What about you, Sunshine?' says the policewoman to the obvious troublemaker, who is me.

'I have been called handsome,' I say.

'Yeah, but you're past your best. Get off the street.'

I turn to the man in the suit.

'Did you say building store?' I say.

'I sell supplies to local builders,' says the man in the suit.

'Really? If you really want to be charitable, I am in real need of a large drill. I need to nail someone to the floor.'

25

NATHAN AT THE HOME
OF ALEX MCGRATH

Here I am again, standing in another damned doorway. I watch Alex McGrath close his eyes and fall backwards through his front door towards the floor. His collapse is not unexpected because I have just hit Alex McGrath on top of his bald head with a two-foot pole that is three inches thick. So there is cause and effect. I know; I hit some other bald person on the head in the Green Onion. Perhaps it is habit forming.

Although his knees buckle, Alex McGrath recovers before he hits the floor. He lurches towards me. I consider this to be threatening behaviour and I hit him again with the pole. I crack the wood against his knees. This halts him, and he screams which is always satisfying to hear but I am not convinced that even with the element of surprise and a very big stick that I am the equal of Alex McGrath. I shoot him in his right foot. My gun was hidden behind my back, so Alex McGrath is shocked. Actually, he is indignant or that is my impression. He says nothing although his mouth is wide open, and this time he is successful in reaching the floor. I step through the doorway, push Alex McGrath clear of the door by kicking his feet. I do this quite gently because, of course, one foot is bleeding rather badly. Alex McGrath makes noises but still says nothing. The prospect of violent reprisal always makes me insecure and impatient, characteristics, which, as we all know, do not help quality decision-making. As well as that, I have the universal need for symmetry. I shoot Alex McGrath in the other foot. McGrath is wearing shoes, so I am spared grotesque effect.

Indeed, the sight of two holes in his sturdy shoes settles me and, with the hand that holds the two-foot pole, I now drag Alex McGrath across the wide floor in his hall. His bruised bald head rests on my hand and the two-foot pole. The scene is almost Native American retreat. His trailing feet leave a smudge of blood on the polished wooden floor.

We arrive in a large and luxurious kitchen that is, frankly, self-indulgent. The kitchen has a large table and six chairs. There are shiny cupboards everywhere and an oven that is big enough to sleep in. Inside the kitchen, I let go of Alex McGrath. I am tempted to hit him again with the pole but the two bullet holes in his feet have reduced the man considerably. He lies on the floor without moving, sometimes staring sideways at me and sometimes at the ceiling above him. His breathing is rapid and deep.

'At the moment you will probably survive,' I say, 'but if you do or say anything in the next few minutes that I deem offensive I will kill you. I will shoot you again but somewhere fatal. I want you to sit in the chair.'

Alex McGrath says nothing but he is no longer curious about the ceiling. He watches me and waits.

'I am not going to lift you,' I say. 'I don't trust you.'

I have a strong rope draped over my shoulder. I look a little like a mountain climber. The rope and the two-foot pole I bought from the man in the suit whom I met in Chester. Alex McGrath noticed and mentioned the rope before I thumped him on the head with the two-foot pole. I remember him at the time saying, 'What the fuck?'

Now, lying on the floor, looking up at me, he says, 'I can't move. I have a lot of pain.'

'I'm obliged to deem your unwillingness to move as offensive,' I say.

I put the rope down on the large kitchen table. The six chairs have tall backs and heavy wooden frames.

'If you sit in a chair, I'll make you a cup of tea,' I say.

Despite other pressing concerns, I am curious about the available luxury. This could be the largest refrigerator door that I will ever open.

'I have a lot of pain,' says Alex McGrath.

'I'll drag you to a chair and you can lift yourself up,' I say.

Alex McGrath says nothing but he is already thinking about vengeance. This is obvious from the look in his eyes. He can think what he wants because I am unreachable.

'You have a problem, Alex,' I say.

'You have left me with a lot of pain,' he says.

He is no longer looking at me. Alex McGrath lies flat on his back and stares at the ceiling.

'Your enemy is willing to self-destruct completely,' I say. 'I am beyond vengeance. My supremacy will be short lived but I feel blessed.'

'I don't know what you're talking about, Nathan,' he says.

'No, I realise that. It is so easy for people like you to make the rest of us only say what you can understand.'

'This pain I have. Phone someone for help.'

'Crawl over to a chair, and I will think about it.'

I watch Alex McGrath drag himself to a chair close to the kitchen table. In the circumstances, he does well. He moves slowly but the groans are minimal. He rests flat on the floor with his head touching the leg of a chair. I pull him up so he is sitting with his back against the legs of the chair. I mellow. I wonder if I am capable of sustained viciousness. If I can do this, I can pull him on the chair, I think. His T-shirt is crumpled and his stomach is exposed. The T-shirt says more than normal. ALEX MCGRATH SUPPORTS ADBURY ANIMAL RESCUE FOUNDATION.

'Get me my cigarettes,' says Alex McGrath.

'I will leave them out for the ambulance men,' I say. 'You can ask them when they arrive.'

I lift McGrath up and put him on the chair by wrapping one arm and the two-foot pole around his neck. With my other hand,

I point the gun at the head of Alex McGrath. The effort exhausts Alex McGrath, and I pretend to let him rest but really I am waiting for him to be ready to do his next task. When he is settled, I drop the strong rope in his lap.

'Tie yourself up,' I say.

'Make me the cup of tea,' says Alex McGrath.

'I've decided against. You having to go to the toilet is not a good idea. '

Alex McGrath stares at the coiled rope in his lap.

'You guessed it,' I say, 'judgement day. If you tie yourself to the chair, I will leave.'

'The pain I have is serious,' says Alex McGrath.

'The sooner you tie yourself, the sooner I can call the ambulance, and the sooner they can arrive and dope you with morphine.'

Alex McGrath lengthens the rope and tries to wrap it around the chair. He is hopeless. Admittedly, his heart is not in it.

'I will tie the rope,' I say. 'But one move, and I will kill you. I am being friendly, Alex. Do not change my mood.'

He lets me tie the rope. I stay behind him at the back of the chair. I put the gun in my waistband, and the two-foot pole lies on the floor behind me. Either there is no fight left in Alex or he has calculated that I am his best chance of survival. Tying him to the chair takes longer than I expected. Finished, I am now impatient to leave but I show him my mobile, which I have inside my jacket pocket. I step outside and I take a hammer, nails and drill from the boot of the Fiesta. I walk back into the kitchen and I put them all on to the large kitchen table.

'Necessary equipment to nail someone to the floor,' I say.

'I have serious pain,' says Alex McGrath.

'I have bruises.'

'This is really serious pain.'

'It has to be, Alex. You interfered with my fate.'

Alex says nothing but he stares at what is lying on the table.

The nails, hammer and drill are large. Only the best had said the man in the suit.

'And now I will interfere with yours,' I say. 'You said you would nail me to the floor.'

'I never intended. I only wanted to put you in your place. You're as bad as Esther. I was only teasing her, Nathan.'

'She shouldn't be dead, Alex.'

'Nathan, see sense, I did not kill Esther. I should not have this pain.'

'You vandalised her home and New Beginnings.'

'I did not, Nathan. She's a woman, Nathan. I'm not going to treat a woman badly.'

'You used to thump your wife.'

'That's different. Nathan, I'm in a lot of pain.'

'You tried to hound Esther out of Adbury with phone calls.'

'I did not. If we met, I would wind her up. She assumed it had to be me. God, she annoyed Carl more than me. He was the one who wanted to see the back of her. He hates anyone rocking the boat. Take my shoes off, Nathan, I have pain.'

I would prefer the shoes stayed on but I am also curious. As I remove the shoes of Alex McGrath, my hands brush against the coarse rope tied around his legs. The shoes are already soggy from the wounds but his feet still drip blood on the polished wooden floor. I remove his socks, which are soaked in blood. Looking at the two bullet holes, I am surprised Alex McGrath has not made more noise.

'Esther had a past, Nathan,' says Alex McGrath. 'Think differently, Nathan, think about someone from outside Adbury. We were a quiet town before she arrived. I have a lot of pain, Nathan.'

'They'll soon be wheeling you through hospital corridors as if you are the most important person in the world,' I say.

I take time to think about it all. I am baffled because it appears to me that nobody has any reason for killing Esther.

'Get yourself some help, Nathan,' says Alex McGrath.

'So I can be fit enough for you to seek vengeance?' I say.

'I have a lot of pain.'

I pick up the drill but leave the nails and hammer on the large table. I touch the mobile inside my jacket.

'Phone right away,' says Alex McGrath.

'As soon as I walk through the front door,' I say.

I walk into the living room and find cigarettes and a lighter on a small table, which is next to a huge chair that faces the TV. I return to the kitchen and put the cigarettes and lighter down on the large table.

The wounds in his feet are still dripping blood. I try to imagine the pain that Alex McGrath says he has but it is beyond me. There is nothing left for me to do or say so I leave. I walk through the doorway and climb into the Fiesta. The whole visit lasted less than ten minutes. I think about what can be done in a day when you are determined. I telephone 999 and give the address of the emergency that I have created. I am not sure if I have done the right thing. Maybe I should have nailed him to the floor, as I had intended. Part of me wanted to because I thought what the hell. I had put two holes in his feet, and it is a waste to not use them. But I have left a lot of blood in that kitchen and, for the first time since I have known him, Alex McGrath looked like someone called Alex, and all that made me think what the hell as well. Two what the hells is not recommended. Satisfied I am not and I never did open the door of the giant refrigerator.

26

NATHAN AT THE FRIENDLY NEIGHBOURHOOD BANK

Actually, I am not there yet. I pass a sign that says
KIMBROUGH
DRIVE SLOWLY THROUGH OUR VILLAGE PLEASE
I am still thinking about Alex McGrath and the holes in his feet and the unused nails and how odd it is that I can think shooting him in the feet was excessive while having regret about not nailing him to the floor. If he had said more, it would have been simpler. Seeing the two wounds in his feet should have calmed me but they have not. I feel as if aggression and anger are sources that I can inject at will. Like a drunk who needs to drink himself into oblivion, I will inject for as long as it takes, and no matter the consequence.

The small village I drive through is clustered around unimportant crossroads. Puddles litter the small flat village green. World War One casualties are listed on the monument in the middle of the grass. A pond bigger than any of the puddles provides comfort for a few ducks. A small bank faces the village green. Outside the bank is parked a large powerful motorcycle that I have seen before. The building has a small door and small leaded windows. A large dairy factory one mile away ensures the bank remains in existence. Most of the time the bank has no customers.

I park the Fiesta on the other side of the road and at the far end of the village. I have a baseball cap, a pair of dark glasses and a pair of tights that once belonged to Esther.

The small door to the bank is open. Midge Stewart leans against the doorframe and fills the doorway. She chews gum and watches ducks float and pose for anybody who might pass. Midge wears a skirt and cardigan and high heels that flatter the curves in her figure. Her black hair is chopped into a trendy style that suits her twenty-two-year-old face. Midge is considered by all to be cute and attractive. She shivers, rubs her shoulders and walks back inside the bank.

The large motorcycle outside the bank does not belong to Midge. This belongs to Dave who also works in the bank. I know them both which is why I am now drawing the tights of Esther over my face and putting on top of them the baseball cap and dark glasses. I drive around the roundabout at the end of the road and I return to the village. I park the Fiesta next to the large motorcycle. I have never ridden a motorcycle. This will be my only opportunity, I think. I resist the idea. I pick up the drill and the gun and I leave the Fiesta and approach the bank. I can hear Midge inside the bank. She is talking to Dave.

'Those leaves should have been cleared by Christmas,' she says. 'They've been here for weeks.'

The dead leaves on the green are dirty brown. I wait at the side of the doorway and listen more. I am unseen.

'I remember when we nearly won the prize for best kept village in Cheshire,' says Midge.

Dave must be listening or perhaps he is working and ignoring Midge. A car approaches the roundabout at the edge of the village and slows down.

The tights, baseball cap and dark glasses are a little obvious and hardly welcome in a well-kept village that nearly won a prize, so I step inside the bank. Midge is still talking,

'Look at us now,' she says.

I see the back of the head of Midge and I see Dave behind the counter. Dave is older than Midge, slightly younger than me. I do not dislike Dave. He says little but his silence is often wistful. I have previously thought about Dave and his large motorcycle. I doubt if it or anything deliver him ecstasy. Dave counts out cash and puts a rubber band around a collection of cheques. He places them in a drawer. Dave has a big beefy build. The kind of build some women like. Dave plays a lot of sport.

'Some people leave their cars here all day,' says Midge. 'The village has become one big parking lot.'

Dave notices the man wearing a baseball cap, tights and dark glasses and who is standing behind Midge.

'We should qualify for yellow lines,' says Midge. 'We have residents like anyone else.'

Dave says nothing but it is obvious to me that he is thinking about baseball caps, tights, dark glasses and the huge drill that I am holding.

'We don't want it too nice,' says Midge. 'There's nothing stopping you from keeping the village clean.'

Dave stays silent. I should really say something but I find this scene from unpressurised rural life an interesting interlude.

'You'd benefit from some manual work,' says Midge, 'sitting here all day.'

Dave says nothing. For a man who is wearing a baseball cap, tights and dark glasses and carrying a heavy drill, I am remarkably quiet. Midge breathes in deeply. This transforms her figure into something admirable. Dave has become pale.

He says nothing.

I picture Dave cleaning his large motorcycle.

'Are you listening to me?' says Midge.

Dave shakes his head very slowly. Midge turns her head around.

The large drill is old which is why the man in the suit was willing to give it to me for nothing. Midge is preoccupied with the drill but I am holding it close to the end of her nose.

'All be quiet,' I say.

I switch on the drill, and it makes an impressive racket. I push the point of the drill against the old-fashioned counter. The noise of rapid explosions makes Midge jump. The counter breaks and cracks. Small pieces of wood fly around the inside of the bank. One hits the ceiling. Midge puts her hands over her eyes. Giant splinters appear around a jagged hole in the middle of the counter. Dave blinks. He is clearly concerned with what is happening to the building fabric of his workplace. I switch off the drill before it breaks.

Midge moves her hands to cover her ears.

'Dave,' she says.

Dave says nothing and frowns. His face is still pale.

I touch the face of Midge with a finger. She wrinkles her nose.

'You,' I say. 'What makes me special?'

'We're frightened of you,' says Midge.

The answer is not unacceptable but I offer an alternative.

'I've got a baseball cap to go with the drill,' I say. ' I'm authentic.'

'You sound authentic,' says Midge.

'You have to move.'

I touch her face again with my finger. Another day, and in different circumstances, I could find consolation in the company of Midge. No chance now, I think.

'Move,' she says, 'where move?'

'Behind the counter move,' I say.

The nylon stocking sticks to my lips as I speak and becomes damp.

'We can all go behind the counter move,' I say.

I know, the grammar is awful but, in certain circumstances, clarity is everything.

Midge leads me behind the counter. Dave stands up. He is taking longer between breaths. I prod both their backs with the old chipped drill. We all stand together behind the counter. Dave looks out of the open door and probably thinks of himself and his large motorcycle passing by fields. Midge looks up at the ceiling, as if she might be praying. Clearly, they are anxious but I am not sympathetic. They fear discomfort. After today, their fate will be intact unlike mine.

'Dave,' says Midge, 'open the safe for him.'

Dave waits for me to speak.

'Hurry up, Dave,' says Midge. 'Don't be a fool.'

'Do as big mouth says,' I say. 'It's all right if I take the money?'

'There's no need to be sarcastic,' says Midge.

Dave is taking deep breaths and looking very pale. Eventually, the breaths produce words. 'We're a small bank,' he says. 'We don't have much money.'

'I can pull the door to,' says Midge. 'Pretend we're closed.'

'Then come straight back here,' I say.

I want to leave this bank because it is not the end I have imagined for me. But I am surprised that I am also prepared for disaster and intervention from others. Dave and me watch Midge close the door, and, while we wait for her to return, I smile for no reason that makes sense. The tights feel damp on my mouth.

'You stay here,' I say through my damp mouth. 'Me and him are going to open the safe.'

Dave looks to the small room behind the counter. The room has a tall safe, filing cabinets and a small table with kettle, tea and coffee. An orange partition shields the safe from normal view.

'Don't argue with him,' says Midge.

'He's not arguing,' I say. 'He just doesn't think very fast.'

'Dave, get a move on,' says Midge.

'You're best being quiet,' I say.

The building drill points at the floor.

Midge prays to the ceiling again. Dave weighs up the various issues as best he can.

'Dave, open the safe,' says Midge.

I realise that Dave is studying me, the baseball cap, the dark glasses, the nylon tights and the building drill. He no longer looks so pale or shocked. I suspect my disguised face is becoming familiar and normal even though it is unrecognisable. Dave walks into the room behind the counter. He pulls the orange partition away from the safe.

I bark a few final words at Midge.

'Empty the tills,' I say. 'Find a decent bag to put the money in.'

I follow Dave all the way to the safe.

I have been very polite, I think. I imagine Dave and Midge commenting on my sensitive manner when the police interview them. The language of bank robbers is normally quite extreme.

Midge begins emptying the tills. In front of the safe, Dave and me stand shoulder to shoulder. The shiny metal surface reflects our faces, well, the face of Dave and my baseball cap and so on.

'This is the safe,' says Dave.

We look up to see how far up the wall the safe reaches.

'Big, isn't it?' says Dave. 'It belongs in a bigger bank than this. I feel sorry for it.'

I say nothing, and we carry on looking at the safe.

'I want this to turn out all right,' says Dave.

'Why don't you open the safe and shut up?' I say.

Midge shouts through the archway between the counter and the room with the safe.

'I've emptied all the tills like you said,' she says.

'Just wait there,' says Dave.

He turns to face me

'I've tried to do the right thing,' says Dave. 'I haven't made a move.'

'I know you haven't,' I say. 'You've done all right.'

I touch the dial on the safe with my drill.

'That won't go through stainless steel,' says Dave.

Midge is keeping quiet wherever she is.

'Open the safe,' I say.

'I can't,' says Dave. 'I just thought that you should see it, at least.'

'I haven't got the time to be messed around. I'll take your head off with my drill.'

We stop talking. I hear a new voice inside the bank.

'This is ridiculous,' says a strange voice.

'I'm sorry,' says Midge, 'I can't help you. I closed the door because we have a problem right now. No, I can't explain.'

'Midge,' Dave whispers the explanation to me.

I am no more than a face behind a nylon stocking, so I appreciate him being polite.

The voices of the stranger and Midge are interrupted by a few moments of silence.

The new voice inside the bank continues.

'What am I going to do for money?' it says.

'Could you come back in half an hour?' says Midge.

'Come back in half an hour?'

'Best make it an hour.'

'I've never heard the like.'

'It would be best.'

'In an hour?'

'It would be best.'

'You people deserve to be closed down.'

'It's a problem beyond our control.'

I lean a shoulder against the tall safe. Dave and me wait through moments of silence.

'He's gone,' shouts Midge.

'Midge, lock that door,' says Dave.

I am still leaning against the tall safe. Dave smiles at my nylon-smothered face under the baseball cap.

'That was close, eh?' says Dave.

'Open the safe,' I say.

'Nathan, I can't open the safe. I don't think so.'

'You said Nathan?' I say.

'I recognised your voice. Nathan, we played in the same cricket team.'

Do not remind me, I think, another misguided idea.

'I'd open the safe if I could,' says Dave. 'Nathan, your best bet is to get out before anybody notices. Nathan, how can you do this?'

I lower the drill until the tip nearly touches the floor.

'You've got a good job in the police, Nathan,' says Dave. 'We played in the same cricket team.'

'I was too old, Dave,' I say.

I press my hand flat on the shiny surface of the tall safe.

'It must be wonderful, Dave,' I say. 'To put money in one place and just leave it there.'

'Nathan, get out while you can,' says Dave

I carefully place the tip of the building drill on the spot between the eyes of Dave.

'Nathan, please,' says Dave.

Dave crosses his eyes as he attempts to look along the length of the drill.

'In a bad mood, I could drill out your brains,' I say.

Dave turns his eyes away from the drill and glances at the front of the safe.

'Not for what's in there,' he says.

Dave looks again at the drill close to his face.

'I'm a desperate man, Dave,' I say.

'You need help, Nathan,' says Dave.

All this talk of help can wear a man down. Whatever happened to moral hazard? Everybody wants to be a social worker.

'I need the money in the safe,' I say.

'I can see you're not yourself, Nathan,' says Dave.

'Open the safe, Dave,' I say.

A little less curiosity and more action, I think.

'Nathan, I can't,' says Dave. 'The safe has a time lock.'

Dave takes a breath and coughs.

'The safe can't be opened until after we close,' he says.

I pull the drill away from Dave and stop leaning against the tall safe. I let the drill rest against my side.

'Clever, aren't you?' I say.

'Not really,' says Dave. 'The safe is a bit of a relic, Nathan. Think it through. I don't think so.'

I take off my baseball cap and rollback the nylon stocking until it is above my eyes. I imagine that revealed I look more ridiculous than I did disguised.

'Dave, I was going downhill fast,' I say.

'Maybe you should quit,' says Dave.

'Quit what, everything?'

'Quit going downhill.'

'Dave, you don't have a choice.'

Dave thinks about God knows what but he has the wistful look that I remember. I think of him on his large motorcycle, using it to pass the time. I consider his lack of progress in the bank and the transfer request to a larger branch that has no doubt been denied.

'Nathan, let's get you out before anyone realises,' says Dave.

'What about Midge?' I say.

'I'll work on Midge.'

'What about the money in the tills?'

I remove the nylon stocking from my face. The top of my head is itchy, and I scratch.

'You can't take it, Nathan,' says Dave. 'People will realise. I don't think so.'

'I'd have a good weekend.'

'I wouldn't take the money myself.'

'You're not going downhill, Dave. You don't know what I've done.'

'No, I go to bed early. I wouldn't mind going to bed right now.'

Dave studies the drill again. I follow Dave back to Midge who is sitting on a stool close to the leaded front window. Two bags full of money wait on the counter. Midge reads a leaflet about tax-free savings accounts and she swings her legs. The blinds on the two tills have both been pulled down. The blinds are the same colour as the bank uniform worn by Midge.

'I sent our customer away,' she says. 'I closed the door. I've collected the money out of the tills.' Midge smiles at Dave and me and she stops swinging her legs.

'You look different without your mask,' she says. 'You're cute, Nathan. It's like having another person in the room.'

Midge knows my face and maybe my name from when I played in the cricket team.

'Dave can't open the safe,' I say.

'Nathan made a bit of a mistake,' says Dave.

'I'm a desperate man,' I say.

'Nathan is going to go home and forget all about it.'

Midge nods her head and smiles.

'Like it never happened?' she says.

She gazes at the drill that I am still holding. She notices the nylon stocking and baseball cap in my hand. The baseball cap says that the person with the head underneath the cap drinks beer.

'By the time we've put all the cash back, we'll have forgotten everything,' she says.

My head still itches, and I ruffle my hair while I stare at Midge and Dave. If they had both been complete strangers, I might feel differently.

'I have this conviction that I should take the money that Midge has kindly taken out of the tills,' I say.

I also have a feeling that Dave and Midge are not surprised. The drill, baseball cap, dark glasses and the nylon tights imply what I know. The chaos has to continue.

'Give him the money, Midge,' says Dave.

'Nathan, don't be a fool,' says Midge.

'You won't keep your mouths shut,' I say.

'We won't if you take the money,' says Dave. 'Give him the money, Midge.'

Midge sits up and pulls her blouse straight.

'I did tell that customer to leave,' says Midge.

I ignore the remark because I do not want to think it through. I throw the baseball cap and nylon tights into the nearest bin.

'I'll leave my drill here,' I say.

I rest it against the hole in the counter and near the giant splinters.

'At least, you're tidy,' says Midge.

'I once played in this village cricket team,' I say.

'I don't follow cricket,' says Midge. 'I've seen you around.'

'I'm actually from Adbury.'

'You're older than me.'

'I'm older than anyone. I just don't care anymore. Give me the money, Midge.'

'There's about eight hundred.'

'It will pay for a decent weekend.'

'It seems such a waste.'

'Don't feel sorry for me. It's all my fault. Perhaps it's not my fault it's my fault.'

I lift the bags of money off the counter.

'They are a fair weight,' I say.

Midge shakes her head, and Dave moves out of the way so I can pass. I carry the bags out from behind the counter. Dave opens the front door and waits. Outside, the village is still wet but the day has turned sunny. The village lawn glistens, and the wet surface of the pond reflects the buildings around the green. I look back at Midge and say thank you. I nod something similar to Dave.

'Don't spend it all at once,' says Dave.

'I'm not that sure I need it,' I say. 'I'm going straight to hell. Would you like to follow?'

'I'm best holding on here.'

'Not today then,' I say.

Dave smiles sheepishly and watches me carry the two blue bags of money to the Fiesta. When the ducks hear me throw the money in the boot, they decide to paddle in a different direction across the pond. I sit behind the steering wheel and switch on the ignition. The lack of any kind of explosion, fire or smoke disheartens me. The song that plays in the CD player is a song that also disappoints. I wind down the window and shout to Dave who is watching from the doorway.

'Straight to hell?' I say.

Dave says nothing and looks down at his feet.

'There are no happy endings, Dave,' I say.

Dave has the wistful look I remember from when we were young.

'It's worse than that,' says Dave.

He glances behind him at the bank where he is obliged to spend his days. He shrugs his shoulders, and the smile is more wistful than ever. I have the odd feeling that he is sorry to see me leave. We wave goodbye, and I drive away.

27

NATHAN AT
BUCKLAND HOUSE

I am standing at the side of my Ford Fiesta. My chin rests on my two hands, which are flat on the roof of the Fiesta. I look over the roof and towards Buckland House. I am still thinking about what I did in the home of Alex McGrath. The money I stole from the bank is in the boot of the Fiesta and forgotten by me. Part of me thinks I should have nailed Alex McGrath to the floor while the rest frets over the consequences for Alex McGrath from leaving two bullet holes in his feet. Will his injuries be disproportionate to the damage he has done, I ask myself.

I am happy to stand and rest. Despite the strong sun, the winter wind is noticeable. Between the large house and me is a smooth lawn bordered by a low wall with statues of animals in the four corners. The tall hedges are manicured rather than trimmed. The mansion is half ruin but it is possible to walk around inside. The rooms not destroyed are still furnished. I know this from previous visits. The guide, who is talking to the tourists, has previously posed for photographs with me but I was calmer then. I watch her tell the tourists what to expect inside. The guide has a job that I envy, talking all day about Buckland House and what happened to the Taylor-Fielders. Before I was useless, I could have done that job. Behind me are rolling fields that are almost as well manicured as the hedges in front of the house. A modest number of deer stroll around the fields. They are as well groomed as the lawns and hedges. The guide leads the tourists inside the house.

I retreat to inside the Fiesta and travel the half-mile to the lake that is at the end of the drive that separates the front house from the fields and the deer. I stop the car as close to the lake as I can. I leave the Fiesta and walk a hundred yards through quite damp grass to the edge of the lake and the monument. Although direct hits were made on the house, bombs were also dropped close to the lake. The monument has been built around the remains of the bombs that missed the house and it is a large piece of broken bomb casing mounted on to a two-foot high plinth. The fin on the bomb casing is still intact. Smaller pieces of bomb casing lay scattered on the grass around the plinth and inside the small iron fence that protects the monument and surrounds the small area around the plinth. There is a small notice in front of the fence that explains the monument. I find a piece of grass against a nearby tree that is without leaves. I sit and stare beyond the plinth towards the lake, which is quiet. I rest my handgun in my lap. I look around the water, grass and trees and regret never joining the *National Trust*. Because my mood has changed, I think again about the two holes in the feet of Alex McGrath. The strong tree rubs against my back but offers more comfort than I had expected. There is enough sun for the lake to sparkle and enough trees for the scene to be pretty. For all my years in Adbury, I am still unable to distinguish one tree from another. I watch a dark cloud break up and let in more sunshine. The lake slaps against the grassy banks and makes gentle murmurs. I slip my gun into the waistband of my trousers. With my arms free, I suddenly feel much more comfortable, not inclined to think about the bullet holes in the feet of Alex McGrath. The noise from the lake is no louder but it is more obvious than before. It reminds me of children playing quietly. All the fields beyond the trees are flat.

I lean my head back against the ruined tree. I close my eyes, undo the buttons on my jacket and think of the well-dressed ghosts left behind by the bomb attack. I imagine them as I have done before, tiny figures waltzing around inside the depths of my brain. I open my eyes for relief and urge the lake to produce modest waves.

For once, I have a desire to light a cigarette. I note the fact that I never smoked as my final pathetic regret. I watch more waves lap the edge and disappear out of existence. My father had brought me to this spot while I was still a child and he had told me all about the bomb and the slaughter of the Taylor-Fielders. I had stood and stared at what was left of the bomb while my father had sat and smoked and, for once, had appeared to enjoy the real world. I gaze along the complicated horizon and, though I think that a decent view on a sunny day is scant return for inevitable misery and consequence, I still regret not ever joining the *National Trust*. I stare beyond the lake and try to remember which writer had said something similar. My memory is deteriorating by the day which is a concern because so few of my thoughts are original. I put my hand into the grass between my feet. The winter breeze is keeping me cool. I bring the gun out of my waistband and let it rest on top of my thigh. I pull out from my wallet the clipping I always carry. I read my obituary.

'Today, Cheshire Constabulary accepted that its esteemed colleague, Nathan Wrench, has probably been murdered.'

I read no further. I lift my head to hear footsteps approach. The footsteps that stop making a noise are recognisable.

'Don't hang around behind me, Kate,' I say. 'So you guessed, if anyone would.'

I wait until Kate walks around to where I sit. Kate stands close to the side of the plinth and the fragment of the bomb. To avoid looking at Kate for too long, I stare at the lake and the view. In the fresh air, Kate looks younger. She waits with purpose, and I admit to myself that she is admirable. I play casually with the gun to avoid being pitiful.

'I can't see the lake properly,' I say. 'You're in the way.'

Kate is short of breath and angry.

'Nathan, this isn't how I intended to spend my last day in Adbury,' she says.

'You take it too easy,' I say.

'You've led me a right dance. Still, your bruises are healing.'

I touch my face. I have not thought about my bruises since I put the holes in the feet of Alex McGrath.

'What's the gun for?' she says.

'Whatever I want,' I say.

I put away my obituary. I had hoped to enjoy reading it with a final relish but there is always someone who interferes. I am not bitter. Why should I be? I can remember every word.

Kate smiles at me. She suits the countryside, perhaps she wears special durable make up.

'Do you do what you want, Kate?' I say.

Kate puts her hands in the deep pockets of her overcoat. She appears to be a person without any problems. She is standing smartly dressed and has a purpose built landscape to frame her face and glory. I reckon she is as confident and elegant as the tiny Taylor-Fielders that waltz around my brain. I rub my back against the tree until it hurts. Not that long after my father had died, I had copulated with a girl against this tree. The girl had never satisfactorily explained why she had let me. The memory helps me think of Esther and her skin, smell and breath. Everything you love either vanishes or perishes, I once read. I did not love Esther, so I stare at Kate. Everything perishes because we all have to leave something, someone and somewhere. Who or what is leaving whom? Who cares, I think. The broken cloud reveals enough sun for it to leave the shadow of the tree across the face of Kate. The sunshine around the shadow is distinct and sharp.

'I haven't come to harm you, Nathan,' says Kate. 'You need help. We have to move forward.'

I draw up my knees and rest my chin on them. The gun slides into my lap.

'You are here to rescue me, Kate? I half hoped you might,' I say.

'I thought you might come here. I expected to see you inside the house. Nathan, it's such a pleasant day. This shouldn't be happening.'

'Don't let the tasteless tranquillity deceive you, Kate. Who said that? God, I can't remember anything. Who said that?'

'I don't know.'

We both stare at the gun in my lap.

'Don't do anything stupid, Nathan,' says Kate.

'You've read that in a manual,' I say. 'Perhaps that's why you're here, to rescue me.'

Kate hesitates, not sure what to say.

I shake my head and rub my chin against my knees.

'You poor creature, Kate,' I say.

'This isn't right,' says Kate. 'You here like this, Nathan. You were going to be the star of the show.'

'My lack of progress really disappoints you, doesn't it, Kate?'

'You've got problems, Nathan.'

'I'm haunted but I'd hate not to be. At least my guardian angels must still be interested. Least, I assume they are.'

'You need help.'

'Perhaps I do but I'm past it. I'm ready to perish.'

Kate edges forward a step.

'Lives do get rebuilt,' she says.

'Shut up, Kate,' I say. 'You have these phrases written down in a note book.'

'That's not fair,' says Kate. 'I do my job. What have you been doing?'

'Recently I've been trying to be a guardian angel. I thought I might as well do something different, a bit of fun. That is all I really wanted. To be just good enough to qualify as a guardian angel of someone after I died. I shot Alex McGrath in his feet.'

'I've been told. I've wasted so much time today.'

'You'd never have caught him. Because of me, Esther is dead.'

'Says who, Nathan? Let's get in the warm.'

'No, Kate.'

'Nathan.'

'I'm not Nathan anymore. I'm no one. No one I want to be.'

I stop talking because I think I have revealed enough. I lift the gun from my lap and rest it on my knees.

'You look well, Kate,' I say. 'It's good to see you in the best of surroundings.'

'I can't relax,' says Kate, 'unless you throw the gun away.'

'No chance, Beautiful.'

Kate and me both sigh at the same time.

'You used to like working for the police,' says Kate.

I study the gun in my lap.

'If I did, it was only when I was young,' I say. 'I kidded myself I was a hero. But you get old, Kate. It's not possible to pretend anymore. And I'm too old to be a rebel. What do you have, Kate?'

'Decent reasons I hope,' she says.

'If the hope inside you goes, what do you do? I have no one to impress and, if I did, it would be beyond me. Do you know what I mean, Kate?'

'No, Nathan.'

'It's simple arithmetic, Kate.'

Kate says nothing.

'You poor creature,' I say. 'Who said you only succeed by imitating your executioners?'

'I'll let you tell me,' says Kate.

'I can't remember. I can't remember anything.'

'Nathan, you're bound to be tired. If you get a proper way of living, sleep and some exercise.'

I lift my head and take the gun off my knees.

'No, this way there's less shame and embarrassment,' I say.

I put the gun in my mouth. The metal helps me taste the fillings inside my teeth, and the sight on the barrel scrapes the roof of my mouth.

'For Christ sake, Nathan,' says Kate.

I take the gun out of my mouth.

'I'll have to say a few words,' I say. 'I'm that type of person. Kate, you're a handsome lady and, though we'd never have been happy, I dedicate my life to you.'

I put the gun back inside my mouth.

'You poor creature,' I say, 'just like your executioners.'

I wink and smile. I feel free of stress, long since unable to impress Kate, I am willing to admit defeat. I push the gun further inside my mouth. I clench the gun between my teeth but am able to speak. The mumble is peculiar but audible.

'"The stroke of a dagger is a caress beside the throb of hopeless days",' I say. 'I can't even remember who said that.'

'Nathan, please,' says Kate. 'Don't break my heart.'

I know that this is beyond me but I am happy to imagine her bereft as a possibility. I am aware that the grin on my face has twisted into something cruel.

'I can't watch,' says Kate.

Kate puts her hands to her eyes. I press my thumb against the trigger and think of what is around me. I am happy to make it all disappear. I hear Kate scream.

28

KATE AND HER FINAL RUN IN THE CHESHIRE COUNTRYSIDE

Kate did her usual stretching exercises to loosen her hamstrings. The exercises made no difference, and her legs were heavy and resistant. She thought about the time in the future when her knees would need support bandages. She shone the powerful torch on her wristwatch. The beam lit up her watch and created a white circle around her on the tarmac. Kate stood by herself in front of the hotel at the edge of the car park. She waited for a guest to leave. While the in-car stereo played a tinkly jazz piano, a BMW dragged a guest out of the car park. The night air was cold on her face and legs. The sky was normal black, and the fields around the hotel were hidden by darkness.

Kate was pleased with the torch although it was really too heavy to carry on a run. For comfort, she squeezed the thick rubber casing. The second finger on the watch climbed to the top of the dial. Kate took deep breaths of the cool night air. She looked down at her feet. Her running shorts reached her knees. She wore gloves and a woollen hat.

The second hand reached twelve, and Kate set off across the car park. She pointed the torch out in front. She ran the same route as she had the night Nathan had followed her. The beam from the torch moved happily from side to side like a friendly dog without a lead. She soon left the car park, and the soles of her trainers slapped against the wet road. Puddles existed where the path had aged and subsided. Kate deliberately splashed through them. She held the torch close to her waist. Trees passed by, and Kate ignored them. She preferred puddles and the road that stretched ahead.

Her breathing became easier. Her stomach was neither sore nor queasy, and, since she had begun sleeping nights again, the skin around her eyes no longer felt tight. Kate always enjoyed the moment during exercise when confidence finally prevailed over anxiety. She lifted the torch so the beam reached further ahead.

Her body, though, felt heavier from the excessive hotel food, and she worried that the lack of sleep from earlier nights might take its toll later. The black sky helped her remember lying in bed in her hotel room, trying to sleep and thinking about the darkness pressing against the windows behind the curtains. Kate pictured a needle in a gauge falling backwards, like an aeroplane dial in an old black and white movie.

The torch in her hand became heavy and awkward. The beam failed to reach as far as before, and her arm felt clumsy. Kate had the daft idea she was beginning to run faster than the beam. She lifted the torch and ignored the cramp around her elbow. Her stomach felt strange again. Not sick just strange. The trees that appeared and disappeared looked wrinkled and alive, as if they expected conversation. The queasiness in her stomach turned into mild pain. Before her body had begun acting strangely, Kate had assumed ageing merely meant her appearance would deteriorate. Kate had told her mother that everything about the body of a woman involved waste and mess; birth, puberty, periods and the change. No wonder modern women preferred plastic faces and milk-less breasts. Her mother had told her not to be disgusting.

Kate cut a corner off the road. She followed the signed footpath through the forest. In the extra darkness the torch was even more effective. Like a dog on a lead, the beam led the way with determination but differently from the kind of dog that moved from side to side. Kate checked her watch and calculated that her running speed was slower than normal. The run on the path through the forest, though, passed more quickly than she expected. Kate rejoined the road. Out of the forest the beam spread sideways and the brightness dissipated into something dull. Kate switched the torch to her left hand and appreciated the relief immediately.

She ran the next half-mile considering whether a contraption could be designed that would support the torch and leave her hands free. She was already beginning to think of a name for the invention and to fantasise about a patent number when she noticed the car parked ahead. As she approached the vehicle, the beam from the torch exposed the heads of two people sitting in the car. Kate saw only the backs of the heads. She ran past the car quickly and stepped through more puddles. Her left arm carrying the torch tired more quickly than the right had. The beam became less disciplined and wandered as far away as the trees at the side of the road. She passed the torch back to her right hand and regained a degree of control. Kate kept running. The road no longer had a pavement. Occasionally, she stepped into the grass at the side. Each time, her fingers would dig into the rubber casing on the torch.

Kate heard the sound of a car engine. She carried on running. She heard the car arrive behind her and felt the light from the powerful headlights crawl over her. She watched the light initially provide company for the beam from her torch. Soon the light, like a whale with smaller fish, swallowed the beam from the torch. Kate ran away from the bright light. She dodged the puddles that appeared but did it without any pleasure, as if she was now obliged to show that she was responsible and formidable. The beam from the headlights crept forward a little. Kate felt afraid. She looked over her shoulder. The car looked bigger than before. The shape behind all the light was vague but more substantial than a shadow. Kate listened to her heartbeat. The ribs nearest to her heart ached more than the others. Her breathing had changed since she had seen the car with the two people inside but her second wind remained intact. She puffed out her chest and ran. She thought about jumping over a hedge and heading for one of the more decent trees where she could fight it out, somewhere authentically rural where it would be inappropriate to be flattened by the car behind.

Kate hoped he would act stupidly. She let the torch point down by her feet and realised she was now carrying it as a weapon. Kate wanted the car to give a warning of some kind, a noise like a gear change, a hesitation in the engine or even a mysterious click. Kate remembered walking in the Yorkshire Moors with her father when she was a child, remembered giant cows staring at her silly walking boots. She was always ready to bolt for a wall at any hint of movement from the cows. Even then she was daft enough to think that her determination would make a difference.

Kate ran towards a modest hill. She made more effort, and her body became warmer. The car moved closer and made a louder noise. The car slowed and rested. Not even a change of gear, thought Kate. Her nose detected the smell of diesel petrol. The hamstrings at the back of her legs tightened. Kate told herself that the pain behind her knees would either go away or move to somewhere else. Kate arrived at the top of the hill. Her breathing became less complicated as she ran along a flat road again. Despite the pain at the back of her legs, she ran with confidence. Kate convinced herself she was running at a decent speed.

The deliberately anonymous tone rang on her mobile phone. Kate pulled the phone out of her tracksuit top. She put the phone to her ear.

'I'm in the middle of a run,' said Kate.

'I know you are,' said Carl.

'I have to do my six miles.'

'I can see you.'

Kate ran a few yards without talking, waited for a decent breath. She looked over her shoulder. The headlights dazzled her eyes. She saw the two shapes behind the windscreen for less than a second. Kate kept running. She avoided the puddles because it was not difficult. In the dark the drenched fields looked dry.

'Carl, you shouldn't be following me,' said Kate.

'I was worried,' said Carl.

Kate looked behind her but saw even less than before.

'You're daft running in the dark, Kate,' said Carl. 'Any woman is.'

She noticed the pain behind her knees again.

'I don't like this, Carl,' said Kate.

The car edged closer.

'It reminds me too much of Nathan,' said Kate,

'Our friend, Nathan,' said Carl. 'We know what happened to him.' He laughed.

Kate turned and stared at the car again. The Mondeo belonged to the police. Surrounded by light, it looked enormous. The headlights hurt her eyes. This time, having to turn her head away annoyed her.

'People used to say me and Nathan were bookends,' said Carl.

'Not me, Carl,' said Kate.

'You were always nasty, Kate.'

'I said you were harmless.'

'You called me General Retard.'

The phone went silent. Kate was aware of the phone lying against her flat damp hair.

'I shouldn't have said that,' said Kate.

'I found out,' said Carl. 'You think I'm stupid.'

'I admire the way you look after your mother.'

Kate was tempted to walk and to save some effort.

'Me and Nathan were both round the bend,' said Carl. 'He knew and I knew and my mother knew. My mother never flattered me. She never said anything decent about Nathan, either. But she liked you, Kate. She's with me now. Don't worry. It's all right, Kate. She's fast asleep.'

'Carl, please overtake,' said Kate. 'I'll see you back at the hotel.'

Kate was more fed up carrying the torch than holding the phone. Her fear was beginning to feel familiar and normal.

'Carl, I'll be no more than thirty minutes,' she said.

She smelled diesel fumes again. The Mondeo was close enough to make a difference to the cold air. Kate straightened her back to see if it would ease the stiffness in her knees. She heard Carl press the brakes on the Mondeo. The fact that he reacted pleased her. She took the mobile phone away from her ear so he would have to wait. She put the phone back to her ear.

Kate kept running. She lifted her feet higher and she was aware of the panic alarm in her knee length shorts slapping against her *thigh.* Kate stepped on to the pavement that appeared on her left. The Mondeo almost came alongside. The pavement felt like an improvement in her circumstances. Not that much of an improvement, she thought.

'Are you going to run me down, Carl?' said Kate.

'I would if I had any sense,' said Carl.

Her running speed had reduced significantly. Kate had the horrible feeling that she resembled the old wrecks that jogged at walking pace. The phone against her ear was causing her neck to ache.

'I'm going to beat you and hurt you,' said Carl.

'What about your mother?' said Kate.

Carl looked sideways at the wrinkled face of the old lady sitting next to him. Carl had insisted his mother wore a woollen hat.

'She'll sleep through anything,' he said. 'I'll drag you away first.'

Kate stopped running but walked as if she was in a rush.

'And then I'm going to kill you,' said Carl.

'You won't be able to tell them this in the canteen,' said Kate.

She concentrated as best as she could. She drew her eye along the hedge at her side above the pavement. She calculated how long it would take to clear the hedge and find a tree and how long it would take Carl to react. The paving stones passed under her feet and reminded her that she was hesitating. The hedge turned into a dry stone wall. The headlight beams helped her see the cracks between the stones.

Marvellous, thought Kate.

'I could run you over if I wanted,' said Carl. 'I hate all this fuss. If it had just been me and Alex, this would have been a quiet town.'

The top of the stone wall looked higher than the previous hedge. Kate felt cramp in her hip. The pain was on the same side that she held the phone. Apart from the hip, she still had pains in her stomach and knees.

'I've always liked women with ambition,' said Carl. 'Now probably not as much as years ago.'

'It's still nice to be wanted, Carl,' said Kate.

'It's not nice at all.'

The Mondeo slowed down, and Carl changed into a lower gear. The engine used a deeper voice. Kate imagined she heard definite hunger. She listened to Carl breathe through the phone.

'Kate?' said Carl

'What, Carl?' said Kate.

'Kate, have you read your letter from Esther yet?'

'I haven't really had time, Carl.'

When Kate talked, the pain in her body increased.

'Have you looked, though?' said Carl.

'I had a quick look,' said Kate.

She looked sideways at the stones on top of the wall.

'So you know,' said Carl.

Kate said nothing.

She used the top of the wall to run a straight line. She thought about whether it would be difficult to jump the wall and whether she would hurt herself.

'We can read it together, Carl,' said Kate.

'I don't think we can, Kate,' said Carl. 'I think I'd be uncomfortable.'

The tree ahead was solitary and enormous. The bare branches reached over the wall. Close to the tree a stone was missing from the top of the wall.

Kate did not hesitate.

She ran and jumped at the point where the missing stone should have been. Kate fell on to the top of the wall, and one of her elbows crashed against a perpendicular stone. She screamed as her knees banged hard against the wall. The phone and torch fell away from her hands and landed in the grass on the other side. Kate was convinced she could hear Carl laugh, could hear crackle and scorn erupting from a twisted scowl. Below her the fallen torch spread light across the grass.

Kate scrambled over the wall and fell down besides the torch.

The light from the torch was bright and it appeared to magnify the scratches and bruises on her knees. Kate clutched the torch and crawled behind the light and along the grass to the foot of the solitary tree. She climbed to her feet, leaned her back against the tree and lifted the torch to point it at the Mondeo. The shape of the vehicle was as visible as a clear outline. Kate held on to her stomach because she felt sick.

She spoke to her stomach.

'Don't you dare,' said Kate.

Her stomach kept quiet.

Kate bent forward and shone the torch on to the different bruises and patches of scraped skin. Across her broken fingernails the varnish had cracked open into a general mess. She put her hand into a pocket in her shorts and wrapped her fingers around the small panic alarm. She noticed that light rain was falling. It tickled the back of her neck and felt like very pointed spongy needles.

Carl stopped the car a few yards ahead of where Kate had jumped the wall. He left his sleeping mother inside the car. He left the headlights switched on and stepped out of the Mondeo. Kate watched him walk and stop behind the stone wall. His walk took some time. He rested an elbow on top of a stone and, with his other arm, shielded his eyes from the light of the torch.

'Kate, take the torch out of my face,' he said.' 'It hurts my eyes.'

She lowered the torch and lit up the wall below Carl. She felt light rain land on the back of her hand.

'This is very messy, Carl,' said Kate. 'You don't want another dead body.'

'It's been a mess for some time, Kate.'

'If it wasn't raining, it would be quite pleasant.'

'Keep that torch low.'

'It is. Who wants to see your tomato face?'

'My mother always says that in the end courtesies are more important than achievements. I can't help being what I am but at least I'm friendly with everyone.'

Carl leaned on the stone wall. Kate looked as far as the Mondeo, through the side window and at the passenger. Not able to see her properly in the dark, Kate imagined a frail old figure dressed in clean clothes and snoring.

Carl looked over his shoulder towards his mother and laughed.

Kate counted to ten and avoided looking at the small human shape in the car. The pain in her side disappeared but her stomach was still queasy, and the cramp felt like a mild groin strain. She counted to ten again. The cramp in her stomach eased a little. She thought about the old lady safe in her seat belt.

Kate lifted the torch.

'That's in my face,' said Carl. 'Kate, I'm coming over the wall. Don't try anything stupid.'

'I'm tempting you,' said Kate, 'if you're man enough.'

'You're going to let me. Just for the sake of a few minutes. You piece of trash.'

'That's right. Come over the wall, Carl.'

Kate thought about the panic alarm in her hand. She took her fingers away and pulled her hand out of her pocket. She beckoned Carl forward with the fingers that had gripped the alarm. She winked and smiled. If she had been years younger, she would have risked something obscene.

Carl straightened his arms and levered himself over the wall. He rested the gun flat on top. Kate waited while he lifted his right foot on to the top of the stones. Carl looked down and checked the foot hanging behind the wall.

Kate threw the torch at Carl and ran not knowing if the torch had hit him or not. She saw the torch bump around the grass and shoot light everywhere. She leaped at the wall again and grabbed Carl around the neck. He caught her head with the butt of his gun but she was able to pull him over the wall. The two of them fell together. He screamed and threw punches. Kate felt one land on her face. She ignored the pain and kept hold. She pulled on his hair and slammed his head into the stone. She did it again. The first time was the hardest *because he struggled more. She heard the gun explode, and, although the side of her body felt the heat from the explosion, the bullet disappeared into nowhere. Fortunately, her blows had weakened him, and she was able to slam his head into the wall again. Kate kept banging his head against the wall until she was tired and until Carl made no resistance and until she felt his blood pour over her hands.*

She let Carl fall out of her hands and on to the damp grass. Her clothes were wet and they stuck to her skin. She lifted up her head so the rain could clean her face. Carl lay flat on his back and was moaning but she put a foot on his chest to be sure. The gun lay in his hand but his grip was loose. Kate bent down and took the gun away from him. She pointed the gun at his bloody head. Very slowly he put his hands to the back of his head.

'I thought you'd let me get over the wall, Kate,' said Carl.

29

NATHAN IN HIS LOYAL
FORD FIESTA SOMEWHERE

I am driving my Ford Fiesta again. I am the Mortal Shuffler, the Flying Dutchman of Cheshire and I am heading to see my Pandora. Actually, I am driving along a country road in Cheshire, the same route that Kate took the night I followed her back to her hotel. I am still alive because I was unable to pull the trigger. Not because I was in the mood to live. If I had been alone, I would have ended it at the lake by Buckland House but when Kate screamed, 'don't break my heart,' I decided against being hasty. Although we hugged afterwards, I have no illusions. I am incapable of breaking the heart of anyone, especially Kate. But I am now the Mortal Shuffler or the Flying Dutchman. Wait until I tell the kids. Now, ahead of me, is a Mondeo police car, and I have no regrets about not pulling the trigger.

The door for the driver has been left open. The lights are switched on, and I can see in the passenger seat a frail figure sleeping with her head against the window. This, I assume, is the mother of Carl. I park my car right behind the Mondeo and look inside the car to check that the person in the passenger seat is sleeping and not dead or injured. The mother of Carl looks quite contented. She snores while her brain is invaded by the dreams of the demented. I walk over to the wall. My Pandora is standing on the other side. Carl is lying on the grass. Pandora pulls a string of cotton away from the edge of her running shorts, and I remember when Pandora heard Carl tell me about his menstrual escapade. The red face of Carl is covered in blood. I climb over the wall because I assume that will please my Pandora.

'Where the fuck have you been,' says Pandora.

'He sneaked through the traffic lights at some road works,' I say. 'I thought I was supposed to keep a safe distance.'

Of course, I should not be here at all. Pandora should have arrested me and taken her prisoner to the police station but, as I had a gun and could outrun her to my car, she agreed that maybe I could be afforded a few more wilful moments. Before I left her at the lake, Pandora told me her plan. As I was beyond her arrest, I suggested that perhaps I could help her. This is why the Mortal Shuffler or the Flying Dutchman, whichever you prefer, and his Ford Fiesta have made this particular stop.

'You were supposed to be here to help me,' says Kate. 'He had a gun.'

Modern policing, I think. It is not all progress for the best.

'I took a chance on you,' says Pandora.

Well, yes and no, I think. I also had a gun, and she was hardly likely to escort me to a police station. Fortunately, I am not the kind of person who always needs to have the last word.

I say nothing, and we both stare at Carl who has stopped bleeding but is making loud groans.

I bend down and pull him up so he can sit with his back against the stone wall.

'I'm fucked,' says Carl.

'We've both had better days,' I say.

The blood on his face has already dried.

'Rest and incarceration is the prescription now,' I say.

Said like that, prison does not sound too unpleasant. Kate, my Pandora, is using a mobile phone while I try and comfort Carl.

'I have to say,' I say, 'I didn't think you had it in you.'

'You thought it was McGrath,' says Carl.

He speaks very slowly, and his voice is quiet.

'I did indeed,' I say.

'You were meant to,' says Carl.

'It all passed me by. I had other concerns, I suppose. You'll have to be careful, Carl. It won't be just rest and incarceration. You'll be a policeman inside with criminals.'

Carl struggles for breath and coughs.

'I wish she'd fucking killed me,' he says.

I stare at the stone wall and notice bloodstains where Kate must have banged the head of Carl against the wall.

'Well, she hasn't,' I say. 'We're both alive. What was going on, Carl?'

'Not now, Nathan, you'll find out soon enough.'

Kate finishes talking on the mobile phone. I think about what motive Carl would have had for killing Esther. Whatever it is, I have no idea. Thinking about motive is a coincidence. While I drove to this spot, I was preparing my defence and thinking that a defence lawyer, saying my actions were irrational and without motive, might just get me a spell in a high security psychiatric hospital. I stand up again so I can look Kate in the eye. She is relaxed and composed but the shorts, woolly hat, trainers and thick stockings do not flatter her. I say nothing. She shivers, and I feel affection for Kate that I thought I had forgotten.

'Carl is not to be moved,' she says. 'We wait for the ambulance.'

We both look down at Carl who actually looks quite comfortable sitting against the stone wall. He certainly looks better than when I arrived. In the car his mother is still asleep. Without Carl the life of her daughter will have to change.

'Let this be a lesson to you,' says Kate. 'The world does not revolve around you, Nathan. And you can fuss and fight as much as you want but you'll never knock it off its axis.'

I look down on Carl and know what she means. I think about Alex McGrath pulling strings and influencing people who should have resisted. But even Alex McGrath was clueless in the end. Nobody controls anyone or anything. We just make a mess. This begrudged nihilism is hardly profound but, considering that I still have no clue what the hell happened with Carl, I am quite pleased that I have retained a certain capacity for independent thought.

An ambulance arrives, and this is soon followed by a couple of police cars. This wakes the mother of Carl, and a policewoman sits down next to the mother inside the Mondeo. They smile and talk about something. The man and the woman from the ambulance climb over the wall and examine Carl. The man wears glasses, and the woman is tall and blonde. She is not beautiful but her presence makes Kate self-conscious.

'We'll need a hand, says the ambulance woman.

We all lift Carl and his stretcher over the stone wall. The bloke who wears glasses and the tall blonde carry him to the ambulance. After Carl is taken inside, Kate points at the stone wall.

'Your turn,' she says.

I climb back over the stone wall and watch the policewoman inside the Mondeo drive away. The ambulance follows the Mondeo down the quiet country road, and both vehicles disappear in the rural darkness. Two uniformed policemen, standing by their own Mondeo, wait for Kate and me.

'Handcuff him,' she says.

I have heard Kate say this before, so it is strange to know that this time she means me.

The uniformed policemen are reluctant to speak, and I have no intention of saying anything to them. In my interrupted existence, I have already wasted too many words on policemen. I will say the minimal although at some point I will have to say, 'I behaved irrationally and acted without motive.'

I say it to Kate as I climb into the police car. I think it definitely sounds all right but she is unimpressed although standing in trainers and running shorts she is obliged to be reserved. I hold up my handcuffed hands so she can see them through the car window.

'Goodbye, Pandora,' I mouth the words so she can understand.

'Take care, Nathan,' she mouths her words as well.

I leave my loyal Fiesta for others.

30

NATHAN IN HIS ROOM IN A HIGH SECURITY PSYCHIATRIC HOSPITAL

I lie on my bed and stare at the ceiling. I am thinking because in my new residence I have ample opportunity. I have spent the morning reading *Armadale* by Wilkie Collins and now I need a break. I like books that have a lot of words. Time goes slowly here but the final day of the trial feels like yesterday. My defence lawyer is prone to claim the credit for everything but in court he used my phrase 'irresponsible and without motive' more than once, and here I am. I have avoided prison. *Daily Mail* readers who become angry about how the money of taxpayers is wasted should look away.

My quarters are in excess of a large mobile home. I have a private bathroom, daily laundering service, a small library that occupies the spare bedroom, a dining room that I use as a study, fully fitted kitchen, wall-to-wall carpets and luxury Cashmere rug, a 46-inch wall hung plasma TV with full subscriptions to Netflix and Lovefilm and a 27 inch Apple iMac. I already have a considerable backlog of books to read but, if any of my orders are not there within the week, my butler is apologetic. He is not really a butler. I just tend to think of him that way. The food is marvellous because three times a day my butler brings in an 'all-you-can-eat-buffet' which rarely repeats previous menus. The breakfast can be routine but only because the choice every day is so extensive. All this exceeds my expectations but once a day, shortly after lunch, my psychiatrist visits me. The woman has developed a fondness and attraction for me, and her visits, which consist of a little psychotherapy, always conclude with serious physical intimacy. She is a passionate woman but she is becoming dependent, and I am aware that could be a problem in future years. But what the hell, I will probably be released in a couple of years, and the psychiatrist will surely keep me satisfied until then.

I am fantasising, of course.

It is true that I have spent the morning reading Wilkie Collins and that now I am thinking. I do have private quarters but they are no bigger than a small room in a cheap hotel. I am comfortable but the bed and pillow share a vengeance against the arthritic. Treatment is actually quite substantial, and my psychiatrist is a plain male, and my describing him as plain might indicate a desperation that I would rather not acknowledge. I do feel guilt, which the psychiatrist thinks is positive, but God do I suffer in the group discussions. I am in the ward for the gentler residents. The mass murderers are elsewhere. But if I hear one more orgasmic description about the merit of arson, I may be tempted to become a killer myself.

But I survive, and co-existence is possible. The psychiatrist calls my fellow patients and me a team. Two of the men are having carnal relations, and I receive regular compliments about my appearance. So I think that it can be said that we have bonded quite successfully.

Kate has visited me once. We talked about Carl but not much. She wore a grey trouser suit and a white blouse. I had my normal uniform but it was clean, and people say I suit blue, well, the men in here say that. We sat in a lounge on normal chairs because I am trusted although a medic waited outside by the door.

'I didn't like making you cry,' I said.

'I don't cry that often,' said Kate. 'I'm glad you're alive.'

'I think you should forget about me and find yourself a boyfriend.'

'I will do that.'

I was not sure what to say. I had not expected my grand gesture to be accepted so readily. It made sense, of course, there was no future for Kate and me although one of us will be useful at the funeral of whoever dies first.

'I know I have been wrong,' I said.

'You know what's right and wrong, Nathan,' said Kate. 'That's why you went crazy.'

'I agonised over McGrath.'

'So you should have.'

'But McGrath was telling the truth. I cannot believe Carl persecuted Esther. He is not the type.'

'Carl throws his weight about with women. He paid women for the privilege, and Esther knew.'

'Carl was taking a chance,' I said.

'He thought he was safe, visiting whores in Leeds. And then Esther arrived in Adbury. She blackmailed him, and Carl thought it a good idea to pressure Esther out of town and pretend it was McGrath. That persuaded Esther to increase her demands. New Beginnings wouldn't pay for the house and BMW.'

'And Esther told you this?'

'Eventually, yes, we did a deal. It was why I hung around.'

'And you told Carl that Esther had written a letter that you intended to read that night which was why he chased you?'

'Anybody else would have sussed me but Carl is a bit thick. Are you reading again, Nathan?'

I nodded.

'You should do a degree,' said Kate.

'Should I?' I said.

'You should do something.'

'Will you come and see me again?'

Kate says nothing, sneaks a look at her phone, which she has under her hand on the table between us.

'If you want, you can,' I said.

'I'm not sure I do,' said Kate.

My ex-wife visited a week later. We sat in the same armchairs that me and Kate had used. She looked okay and said I did. We must both be eating three meals a day. My ex-wife is called Susan. She has kept the name Wrench but that is because of the children, not me.

'The girls want to see you, Nathan,' said Susan. 'If there's anything I and the girls can do to help.'

She showed me a short video of the two girls that she had on the phone. The girls were drinking coffee on an outside terrace in a café in the Yorkshire Dales. I had never seen anything or anyone more beautiful.

When she saw me smiling, she said, 'The idiots think they've failed you.'

'You told them that was not true?' I said.

'I put them right.'

My ex-wife is tall like Kate. The attractiveness of her face owes more to her big eyes rather than refined features.

'How many times did I plead with you to leave the police?' she said.

'I suppose I must have always had the pension at the back of my mind,' I said. 'For a while I was happy enough just hating the police, in the end I hated everyone.'

'The girls want me to give you your books back.'

'I have plenty of books.'

We had argued about who should keep the books. Now it meant nothing.

'Has Kate visited?' said Susan.

'She has been here the once,' I said. 'She told me about Carl.'

'I used to be jealous of Kate. You talked about her a lot.'

'She was not a phoney. It felt like real work when she was here.'

'Phoneys or heroes, that's how you categorised people.'

'We can't be heroes for ever,' I said.

'We've got two kids to worry about,' said Susan

'You said I made things worse.'

'So you did.'

It is only weeks since I saw Susan and Kate but I know neither will visit again. The visits were important because they have made me certain that I must not return to Adbury when this is over.

3 1

NATHAN IS IN THE LIBRARY

I am reading a letter in the hospital library. Not my own library because, despite my fantasies, I do not have one in my single room retreat. I am allowed to withdraw four books, which I can swap at any time. When I begin my degree in English Literature, the allocation will be increased to six. I have just finished using the PC to secure a place on a University course. I was helped. We are not allowed our own email account. I do not send letters to anyone. I am happy that Susan, Kate and my children will forget me. My psychiatrist has told me that I should think about a future career in teaching. This sounds fanciful but I keep myself entertained with hope, which I have not done for some time.

Although I do not send letters, I have received a couple. One is from Carl. This is what he has written.

Mate

How are you doing? I thought it would be a good idea if we kept in touch. I realise that I am not your number one fave rave at the moment but considering how we are both placed I thought I should make the effort to talk. Obviously, the first thing I have to do is apologise.

Mate, I was desperate. The woman was out to ruin me and I suppose that you knocking her off made me resentful towards you especially as you were not exactly being the responsible policeman. I know. It's irrational but a man under pressure and all that. I shouldn't have put the smack into you that night but when I found it in the motor in the garage it seemed as if it was an opportunity. I wasn't thinking straight then and you were out of your head. I have regrets. I wish I could have talked to Esther and made her see sense and I definitely made things worse when I had her house painted yellow. Have to say, though, that those blokes who did it kept quiet until the end. If I told you who it was, you would laugh. And who knows, maybe in the future we will be able to have a laugh like we did in the old days because it wasn't always bad. I sometimes think it is easier in the big cities. In the small towns a couple of people can create chaos. I'm not meaning you. We all know that you had real problems and I only hope that you are getting proper care now where you are. Here, I have to be careful. But I spoke to the warden about me being victimised because I was a copper and he said prison is like social housing and all it needs are the right families on the right streets. I keep a low profile and of course the guards know that after I leave prison more than one newspaper will be willing to listen to what I have to say. I am protected and I do not feel threatened. If anything, I'm surprised just how timid are some of these blokes. I think back and feel a bit off about some of the things I did. I don't mean Esther. She was no innocent and could look after herself. I'm talking about how I leaned on the hopeless though I didn't think of them that way at the time.

My sister is struggling with my mother but is making the best of it. She writes to me regularly because she knows I worry but also because I think it helps her to have a moan or just talk about how crazy life can be. I thought she would abandon me but not because of the killing. That was a man at the end of his tether. I was more concerned about her reading about what I got up to in Leeds with the women that Esther knew. Well, we all have our needs and our dark side and my sister said that women are not as easily shocked as men think. Kate was surprised I travelled to Leeds for my pleasures but you don't do that kind of thing on your doorstep. God knows, I never expected Esther to appear in Adbury the way she did.

My mother thinks I am working abroad. My sister wants my mother to visit here and she thinks if we tell her that I am in hospital then my mother will believe it. Maybe I will be able to see her in a private room.

I do think we should be friends and put behind us what happened. I keep myself busy with keeping fit and I have subscribed to a teach yourself course on how to become a fitness trainer. Alex visited me a week ago and he thinks I might be able to help in the gym at Barrel Park some day but obviously that is a long way off. I should tell you that I doubt if Alex will ever let bygones be bygones. He has two walking sticks these days. So I think it is best if you stay out of Adbury. I am assuming that they will say you are cured in a couple of years and let you out then.

More than anything, though, it would be good if we can become mates again. There might come a time when you might even be able to visit me here.

Anyway, take care and do write.

A mate that always thought that you were too good for the rest of us.

Carl

I have not written a reply. Each time my nerve fails me halfway through the first sentence. But a mate is a mate, and I am pitifully short, so I will reply at some point. I have doubts and I am not sure if Carl only wrote because Alex wanted me to have a warning. The truth is that I have never imagined Carl as a threat. I will not return to Adbury but I can write a letter. It is not likely that I will visit him in prison. Thinking of what to write will be difficult but I will definitely reply. I believe Carl wants to be friends. As the Spanish perhaps say to each other, *el es mi amigo.*

I also have a letter from Kate. I keep the letter from Carl because I need the address. I keep the letter from Kate because something had to replace the obituary I was obliged to destroy. This is what Kate has written.

Nathan

I am sorry that I said so little when I visited. I could blame the hospital environment but I will not. I will never deny that I enjoyed

*our months together but now I feel like I was, whatever you felt for me,
something that you merely had. Some of that, I realise, is because of
circumstance. I was your mistress even though I had you as my lover.
Unfortunately, I am now aware of your nature.*

Kate

I keep the letter from Carl amongst my notes on Buckland
House. I carry the letter from Kate in the breast pocket of my
uniform. It stops me from being light headed.

3 2

KATE ON THE BEACH AGAIN

Every night Kate runs past the metal men.

Now it is the summer, and, after her visit to Adbury, she rarely thinks about Nathan. She saw him once in the psychiatric hospital but will not see him again. In Adbury, Kate and Nathan had lain side by side on the same bed but now it is different.

Now it is the summer, and there is enough late light to see properly the extent of the sea and the horizon. Under this always available summer light the waves sound quieter, as if the echo and meaning previously provided by the darkness was only distortion.

Now Kate doubts if she ever really loved Nathan. Some nights she does remember saying at the lake, 'don't break my heart', but oddly, when she does, Nathan is not in the memory.

Now Kate thinks that what she said to Nathan was mere protest against what will or might happen and that by the lake, seeing Nathan with a gun inside his mouth, was the moment to make the protest but that none of it was likely to be resolved by saving Nathan.

Each night she runs past the metal men and listens to the sound of her footsteps on the wet sand of the beach, and each night she is anxious.

Although Kate rarely thinks about Nathan, she does think about what she said about the world not revolving around one person. But again, Nathan is not in the thought. Instead, Kate thinks about the metal men and how the view that they have is only partial. To every one of them, firm and straight and looking at endless sky and sea, it must appear as if they see everything.

Each night she runs past the metal men.

Now, instead of thinking about whether she ever really loved Nathan, she remembers an existence in Adbury when she had a different view from what she has in Liverpool.

Each night the metal men are the same. The small amount of sand between each of the metal men has consequence beyond them. Sometimes, but only rarely, Kate remembers and accepts that Nathan was important to a certain view in a particular phase of her life.

Now it would be easy for Kate to think that Nathan was no more than mere distortion and interference, something like what happens in the darkness on the beach in winter.

But each night Kate runs past the metal men and sometimes, but only rarely, Kate insists to the nearest metal man that Nathan was not her love but neither was he distortion.

Each night Kate runs past the metal men and sometimes she imagines them all with heart and ill informed hope. These are the moments when she thinks about the future and the consequence for her own heart. These are the moments when she worries that there will always be something waiting to break it.